Jimmy Lagowski
Saves the World

by Pat Pujolas

Published by Independent Talent Group, Inc.
Fairlawn, Ohio 44333
kwilson_itginc@yahoo.com

ISBN: 0984009302
ISBN-13: 978-0-9840093-0-5

LCCN: 2011916242

Cover Design: Steve McKeown
Cover Photo: C.J. Burton

for Jason

CONTENTS

ACKNOWLEDGEMENTS

The author would like to thank the following people for their readership, advice, and super-coolness: Kirsten Bell, Mark Blandford, Gregg Brokaw, Tim Brokaw, Natalie Brown, Sara Buchanan, Marty Burke, James Alex Butler, Aikta Chugh, Laura Cutsey, Gary Dague, Trish DiFranco, Wendy Ducker, Leah Dwyer, Tyler Findlay, Erik Flesher, Brian Gillen, Heidi Hagan Gordon, Rose Gowen, Reid Harrison, Julie Hudson, Wes Jones, Monica Kaiser, Rana Kardestuncer, Jessica Keener, Kevin Kerwin, Ryan Kindinger, Holly Kirby, Sara Koch Krauss, Mike Kolonik, Sue Gilbert Krizman, Laurie Lapinskas, Dave Lewman, Daniella Macri, Nicolas Marin, Marisa Mayer, Mark & Autumn McKenzie, Steve & Anne McKeown, Tess McShane, Tom Megalis, Matt Nelson, Mary Olson, Kate Purdy, Kristin Rhoades, Katie Riley, Willow Rosen, Jeff Shattuck, Scott Sloan, Chris Surak, Dave Thomson, Chris Viola, Malachy Walsh, Chloe Williams, and everyone who visited the "story-a-month" fiction blog. Special thanks to *Connotation Press* (Ken Robidoux, Meg Tuite, Anna March, et al) for their support and promotion of the title story in this collection. Super-duper special thanks to all the major peeps and playas in my life: Bill & Julie Brokaw, Mark Hentemann, Tonya & Ali Higgins, Catherine Locker, my family (Ron & Jan Pujolas, Terri Pujolas, Randy & Nancy Knauer, Beth & Shawn Rapp, the Dooley's, the Rich's, the Murray's, the Yowler's, and the Pujolas's!), my kids (Amelia, Porter, & Sofi), and especially my wife, Kristin Wilson--for her love, kindness, and inspiration; without her, there would be no book (for reals yo).

"All men are created equal."
-Thomas Jefferson

"Thomas Jefferson was a dick."
-Jimmy Lagowski

IN MEMORIAM

One by one, cars filed into the cemetery, pelted by the summer rain under a gun-metal sky. The procession moved slowly, a series of brake lights and headlights, too close together, too far apart; there were sedans and SUVs, mini-vans and pick-up trucks, shiny new vehicles and rusty old ones, held in common only by the small, purple "Funeral" flags atop their hoods.

Inside the cars, the people too were moving slowly, as if drugged or dulled by the weight of it all, the occasion of human death. Drivers and passengers wiped tears from one another's cheeks; some smoked cigarettes or listened to music on low volumes, careful not to betray their composure, the gravity of the moment.

Soon the lead hearse stopped at the foot of a grassy knoll adorned with tombstones and grave markers; at the crest of the knoll stood a rented white canopy; its canvas buckled and swayed in the wind, ballooned against the aluminum frame.

The line of cars stopped; drivers turned off ignitions; headlights and brake lights went dark; windshield wipers froze in place.

For a moment, there was just the sound of the rain, sizzling across the pavement, crackling atop the roofs and hoods of the cars.

Then a door opened at the front of the procession, the lead hearse; the funeral director emerged, raising a massive black umbrella. He waved his hand, signaling the others to get out and come forward.

Umbrellas blossomed from open car doors in various shapes and sizes and colors; beneath the umbrellas came the funeral-goers, wearing dark suits, long dresses, formal shoes; they trudged alongside the line-up of parked cars, occasionally bumping umbrellas, shuffling in a single file line.

The people gathered around the hearse, waited patiently for instruction, while the rain blew in at them from the sides.

At last, the funeral director spoke, "Can I have my pallbearers, please?"

The men came forward, surrendered their umbrellas; these men resembled one another; they were brothers or cousins, blood relatives; the slight differences in size or age could not mask the stark similarities: the wavy black hair, the bulbous noses, the sunken brown eyes.

The pallbearers, standing shoulder to shoulder, eased the coffin from out of the hearse, and found their grip on the brass carrying handles; the funeral director whispered directions to them, then addressed the crowd calmly.

"Everyone, please be careful going up the hill. Some spots are slippery."

And with that, the man led the march up the grassy knoll; the pallbearers followed closely behind him, their suits already soaked by the rain; they struggled against the weight and bulk of the coffin.

From somewhere in the crowd, an elderly woman began to wail; her husband held her closely but could not contain her sobs; the cries became contagious; others began shedding tears as well, men and women equally, as they trudged up the slick, grassy hill.

Nearer to the top, one of the pallbearers slipped and fell to one knee; he got up quickly, wiped a smear of mud from his pant-leg; the other pallbearers paused and re-adjusted their grips on the wet handles; then, with a nod from the man who slipped, they continued on to their destination beneath the white canopy.

Following signals from the funeral director, the pallbearers positioned the coffin above the burial plot and its framework; finally, the pallbearers rested; they huddled together and waited for the others to join them.

The priest was among the first to arrive; he wiped the raindrops from his glasses then removed a magnificent book from a plastic bag; it was a gilded Bible, sheathed in red leather with glimmering gold pages.

The funeral-goers pushed forward, but the canopy wasn't large enough to shelter everyone; so some of the men excused themselves to the perimeter of the crowd, steeling themselves against the rain and the wind.

Employees of the funeral home circulated, distributing freshly cut flowers to those in attendance. Tulips. Roses. Daisies. Carnations. One flower for each person.

From inside the tent, the priest welcomed the funeral-goers with open arms; he asked the people to bow their heads in reverence, then opened the Bible and began reading.

"Let us pray."

As if on cue, the rain began to subside, then

cease entirely; the men outside the canopy were the first to notice it; umbrellas were collapsed; people murmured and shrugged.

The priest's voice was louder now, in the absence of the rain; his words carried easily to the most distant of listeners.

"For as much as it hath pleased Almighty God of His great mercy to take unto Himself the soul of our dear sister here departed, we therefore commit her body to the ground; earth to earth, ashes to ashes, dust to dust; in sure and certain hope of the Resurrection to eternal life, through our Lord Jesus Christ; who shall change our vile body, that it may be liken unto His glorious body, according to the mighty working, whereby He is able to subdue all things to Himself."

Silence.

Then, a gasp. A woman's gasp, pleasant and distinct. Followed by another, a man this time, from outside the canopy. Someone in the crowd pointed upward, toward the sky; and one by one they all saw it: sunshine! Two massive, gray rain clouds were parting, allowing radiant beams of sunlight to pass through unfiltered.

A woman blessed herself, motioning the sign of the cross. Others followed her example; curious men and women excused themselves toward the perimeter, still carrying the freshly-cut flowers; they strained to get a better look. Some people murmured aloud; some smiled; some merely closed their eyes, wondering what this could mean.

Was it a sign? A message of some sort?

The priest waved his hands in the air, tried to regain their attention. "Ladies and gentlemen, what we are seeing here today..." he said, pausing for dramatic effect.

Crack!

A deafening noise.

Like a small explosion.

One of the pallbearers slumped to the ground, his face missing; behind him stood a man dressed in black, holding a gun.

A few feet away, the priest froze in shock, his white robe and glasses now spattered with blood.

The gunman pointed the barrel downward at the fallen pallbearer, and pulled the trigger once more.

Crack!

People screamed; people ran.

Chaos.

In the confusion that followed, some would swear it was the funeral director; others would say it was a dark stranger, or the devil himself; the only thing they would all agree on: the man came from nowhere and left the same way.

People slipped and fell in their struggle to escape; they scrambled to their feet and they ran again, pulling relatives by the hand, by articles of clothing; they took shelter behind grave markers; they hid behind cars and trees; they huddled with family members, protecting them; they prayed and made promises; they survived.

The priest crawled to the fallen man, the pallbearer, and tried in vain to give CPR; it was useless; beside them, all around them in fact, were colorful flower petals and long green stems, trampled into the damp earth.

"Call 9-1-1!" a man was shouting from behind the hearse. "Somebody call 9-1-1!"

"Where is he?" shouted another voice in return. "Where the hell did he go?!"

STATE PARK RESORT

The boy wakes up with a boner to end all
boners. A raging twelve-year-old hard-on. His
sleeping bag is heavy with dew, but the air inside
the tent is already sun-baked and warm. He stands
and stretches, waving the erection from side to
side; curious, he hangs a sock from it, then a
tennis shoe; but none of this helps; it only makes
the boner hurt more. So he sits on the cot and he
waits; he thinks about grandmothers, and dentists,
and the taste of fried liver; he waits, and he
waits, and he waits.

Outside, the boy's father is seated at the
campsite's picnic table, re-reading yesterday's
newspaper; beside him an electric coffee pot
gurgles and gasps; on the table there is coffee
cake, a wet jug of milk, and a few mini-boxes of
sugar cereal.

"Morning, Henry," his dad says.

"Hi."

"How'd you sleep?"

"Okay."

Henry sits on the bench and reaches for a box
of cereal. Using his Swiss-army knife, he saws

through the dotted lines of the small carton,
neatly carving a capital "I." His leg is itching,
a new mosquito bite, so Henry presses the knife's
cold blade into the pink welt. Twice.

"What are you doing?" his father asks, from
behind the sports page.

"Mosquito bite."

"Don't play with it. You'll just make it
worse."

"But it itches."

"I said don't play with it."

Henry rubs the bite with the toe of his shoe,
slowly at first, then faster; soon the whole
picnic table is rocking, and his father's coffee
splashes over the side.

"Henry!" he slaps the paper down.

"What? It itches."

"I told you--" he sighs. "You know what your
problem is?"

Yes, he does. Because these days, people are
always telling Henry what his problem is. Or
asking him what his problem is. Twelve years old,
Henry thinks, the year of the problems.

"Lack of self-control," his dad says.
"Sometimes, it's like you have no control over
your body. Like a clumsy puppy."

"I can't help it."

"You have to learn to control yourself." He
blots the spilled coffee with a napkin.

"I know."

His dad carries the napkin and the newspaper to
the trash can beside the camper. Henry seizes the
opportunity to scratch the mosquito bite with his
fingernails. And it feels so good. It feels better
than good. It feels amazing.

*   *   *   *   *

Afterwards, he sets about climbing the tree again. There is a pattern to this, a formula that only Henry knows. First, you jump up, grabbing the lowest branch of the tree, thick as a cucumber, with both hands. Then you swing your legs, gathering momentum, while you throw your head back and pull upwards; with a good hard kick you should be able to snag the next branch with your feet. And voila! Upward.

Henry climbs and climbs, grasping tree branches like rungs on a ladder. He keeps going, all the way, until the trunk itself begins to sway under his weight. His favorite spot. From the ground, nobody can see him (too many branches and leaves). But from up here, Henry can see everything.

He loves this tree. The campsite too. Nobody has camped in front of them yet, and so they have the entire hill to themselves. To throw frisbees and lawn-jarts. To play badminton and volleyball. To catch lightning bugs. And to build bonfires. This campsite is the spot where all his parents' friends gather to drink beer and tell stories at night; there's the Kowalski's (no kids), the Cannon's (stupid Robbie Cannon), the McAndrews (Mo and Kenny), and of course the Martin's (starring Joann Martin, 16, goddess of Henry's world).

From his back pocket, Henry removes the Swiss-army knife and begins carving her initials into the tree bark. It takes him longer than he expected. He's barely finished with the "J" when he hears his mother's voice.

"Henry? Did you take a shower yet? Henry? Where are you?"

He ignores her, relishing his invisibility status. Instead he returns to his handiwork; before long a daddy-long-legs spider approaches, crawling stealthily down the trunk. Henry pins one of the spider's legs to the bark with his thumb.

Then with the knife, he severs a leg from its body. Then another. The legs fall like eyelashes. "You know what your problem is," Henry tells the spider, "lack of self-control." Then he lifts his thumb from the bark, and the spider's body falls, slowly falls, jerking and tumbling to the ground below.

* * * * *

Inside the shower-house a group of boys his age are up to something; Henry can tell by the way they are whispering, laughing, and pushing each other around. Henry brushes his teeth, while watching these boys in the mirror.

They are taking turns, hoisting each other up inside the shower stalls, trying to peek through an open gap near the ceiling -- into the women's showers next door.

"I just saw some pussy," one of the boys says. "A huge bush."

"Probably your mom's," another boy says. "Burn!"

Henry spits out some toothpaste into the sink, and dries his mouth with a towel. The tallest boy is now straddling a shower stall divider, craning to peer down through the open space.

On the other side of the wall, a woman's voice calls out: "Hey! Get down from there!"

"Shit!" the boy says, grabbing the wall, and scrambling down.

"I'm calling the ranger!" the woman yells.

"Go! Go! Go!" All the boys head for the exit, pushing and pulling away from each other, flip-flops skidding and sliding over wet sandy tiles. Henry steps back, allowing them to pass.

The boys yank open the door, and are gone, gone, gone, laughing hysterically and running for their lives. Outside, the woman's voice calls to them: "Come back here! I'm telling your parents!"

"Screw you, fatso!" one of the boys yells, already far down the road.

And then the bathroom door jerks open again; a large angry woman wearing a purple robe/mu-mu/thing; she points a finger at Henry.

"You spying on us?"

"No, ma'am. I was brushing my teeth." He holds up his toothbrush to prove it.

"I ever catch you spying again, I'll pull down your pants and spank you myself! You hear me?"

"Yes, ma'am," he mumbles.

"Little perverts!" the woman says, closing the door behind her. Henry's heart is racing; his cheeks are hot, and he's holding his breath. Holy crap! And he didn't even do anything! What the heck? Henry grabs his towel and retreats to the shower stalls; he enters the last one and locks the door behind him; then he sits on the wet, wooden bench, thinking. Above him, not more than six feet away, is an open passage to naked women. This, Henry decides, is his newest and greatest secret.

*   *   *   *   *

Walking back to the campsite, Henry spots Joann Martin relaxing in a lounge chair, reading a book; Joann's whole family is there too, talking, eating and drinking. Henry deliberately slows down, angles his path to pass by nearer to them.

"Hello, Henry," Mrs. Martin says.

"Hi," Henry says.

"Hey, Joann," Henry says. "Want to play some badminton?"

"Sure," she says, twisting a strand of long brown hair. "You really think you can beat me?"

"Oh, I don't think I can... I know I can,"
Henry says. Today is the day, he thinks; he will
tell Joann Martin how he feels about her, that he
loves her more than anything else in this world.

Joann gathers the rackets and birdie from under
the Martin's camper. Her legs are long and smooth
and tan, glistening with tiny golden hairs. She's
wearing a green bikini top, white shorts, and
sunglasses with gold frames. When she walks toward
Henry, her flip-flops snap against the soles of
her tanned feet.

"Let's volley for serve," Joann says; her teeth
are white, packed closely together; Henry's own
teeth are yellow and have gaps between them.

"Your funeral," he says.

"You are so funny," Joann responds. And the two
of them begin to play. She easily takes the first
five points, but then Henry discovers a weakness
in her game. Those little "dink" shots where he
barely hits the birdie. Every time, she rushes the
net, breasts jiggling, and misses with the
underhand. Before long, the game evens up. 6-5,
Joann. And then 9-6 Henry. Then it's game point,
Henry's advantage.

This is it, his big chance. "So," Henry says,
"What are we playing for?"

"Excuse me?"

"What are we playing for? A hundred bucks or
something?"

"You are a riot," she says. "We're not playing
for anything."

"But if you could have anything in the whole
wide world, what would it be?" Henry asks.

"I don't know," she says. "A new puppy?"

Not what he was hoping for.

"My brother is allergic, so we've never been
allowed to have a dog."

"Okay," he says.

Henry waits, hoping she will ask him the same question in return; because he knows what the answer will be. But Joann is silent, waiting for his serve, rocking back and forth on the balls of her feet, like a tennis player. Come on, Henry thinks, ask me. Ask me!

"Any day now," Joann says. "While it's still 1982."

*　*　*　*　*

"I don't know. Maybe because it's a lake," his dad says. "The water is too dark, so you can't see when people go under. Or drown."

Henry looks out at the swimming lake, a man-made, oval-shaped body of water with a grassy island in the middle, skewered by a white flagpole. On the far side of the lake is a "deep end" with a concrete platform, diving boards, slides, monkey rings, and a pulley system that takes riders from a 30-foot-high stage down a slanted cable into the murky brown water.

Henry takes a bite of peanut-butter-and-jelly, imagines bumping into a dead body underwater, the feel of its clammy, bloated flesh.

"Awesome," he says.

"Not when you have kids," his mom says. "But your father's correct. That is why they have safety breaks. So people don't drown."

Henry leans back, elbows sinking into warm towel, savoring gobs of grape jelly mixed with salty peanut butter and fresh bread. The Martins are not here yet; right now it's just Henry's family, the Cannon's (and stupid Robbie), and the Kowalski's, who are drinking wine out of a red Thermos jug.

"Where is everybody?" Henry asks, swatting at a bee near his sandwich. The only response comes from the bathhouse's loudspeakers: "Attention swimmers. Safety break is now over. You may now return to the water."

Kids cheer and clap and run into shallow water, splashing and leaping and laughing. Lifeguards wearing red bathing suits and whistles return to their tall lifeguard chairs.

"Stupid bees!" Henry says, standing.

"Leave them alone, and they'll leave you alone," his dad says.

Henry karate chops the bees, kicks at them. "Hi-yah! Take that, bees!"

He accidentally steps on a bag of pretzels, smashing them.

"Ooops."

"Henry, why don't you put on your suit and go swimming?" his dad says. "Use up some of that energy."

"Fine." Henry takes his backpack and marches off toward the bathhouse, through a maze of towels and blankets, beach chairs and coolers, half-naked bodies, and huge metal garbage cans overflowing with candy wrappers, soda cans, bees and wasps.

Inside the changing room, Henry unzips the backpack, takes out the brand new bathing suit, and lays it on the bench. A black Speedo with gold racing stripes down the side. It is, Henry thinks, exactly like the one that cool guy wore in "Caddyshack."

Henry puts the suit on. It feels sleek. And fast! The walls here, he notices, have open vents just like at the shower house. He imagines spying on Joann, watching her change into her green bikini. Then he envisions Joann looking up, catching him spying, his chances blown forever. Nocando, he thinks, stuffing his clothes into the backpack, he heads back to his family.

"So... where is everybody?" Henry asks once

again as he approaches.

"Oh my God!" Robbie shouts, pointing at Henry. "Check it out! Henry's wearing a marble-bag!"

The adults laugh. The kids laugh. Everyone laughs at Henry.

Henry sits on his towel, pretending that he didn't hear anything. But he can feel the blood in his cheeks, the tears coming to his eyes. He wishes for a pair of sunglasses to hide behind.

But mercifully, there is a distraction; heads begin turning in another direction; the girl with one leg is being helped from the water by her father. Henry has seen this girl before, knows her name. Kendra. She's a teenager, and her left leg has been amputated below the knee; there is a knot of skin on the end of the stump; it reminds Henry of a Tootsie roll wrapper.

"Poor thing," Henry's mom says.

"A shark ate her leg, I bet," Robbie says. "Just like in Jaws."

"Robbie," his mom says.

"So sad," Henry's mom says again. "It just makes you realize how good you have it." Henry wipes the tears from his eyes and looks at his father, who is now sound asleep face-down on the blanket, skin ablaze in red and pink.

*   *   *   *   *

Nothing calms him like a good game of Pac-man; because for the most part, Henry knows what to expect (and when); as long as you follow the pattern and never stray from it: left, down, left, down, right (all the way), up, left, up, right, through tunnel, up, right, up, right, down, left, down, right, down, right, eat the fruit, up, right, back through the tunnel again, etc, etc. All of which is precisely why the top three scores on this Pac-man machine belong to "HNR."

But this particular machine is starting to act up again; Henry can tell whenever Blinky gets stuck in the tunnel, pacing back and forth; before long, the energy dots won't disappear when Pac-man eats them. Then there's nothing you can do; the game freezes, and you have to unplug the machine, wait a few minutes, and plug it back in. "A poor man's reset," Kenny calls it.

Henry pulls the cord, then looks at the clock: 7:35pm. Mostly there are only teenagers left, smoking cigarettes and watching Kenny play pool. Kenny's not wearing a shirt, just a denim jacket, with a gold chain around his neck.

"Four ball, corner pocket," Kenny announces. And slam! The purple ball disappears.

"With authority!" someone adds.

Kenny smiles, noticing Henry. "Hey what's up, boss?"

"Nothing much," Henry says, honored that Kenny greets him with so many other teenagers around. "Just hanging out."

"You got a quarter for me?"

"You know I do," Henry says, opening his velcro wallet; he forks over a bicentennial quarter to Kenny. They both know what it's for; Kenny strolls to the jukebox and drops the quarter in the slot.

"Ladies and gentlemen," Kenny says, "My good friend, Boz Scaggs." And like magic, the jukebox comes to life: guitar chords and drum beats.

> *"Lido missed the boat that day*
> *He left the shack*
> *But that was all he missed*
> *'Cuz he ain't coming back..."*

Kenny, mid-story: "So anyways, we're getting all into it, rolling around on the blanket, buck naked, and all of a sudden, fucking security shines his flashlight on us. And he's all like, 'Hey, it's past curfew. What are you doing out here?'

"So I say, isn't it obvious? We're giving you your jollies, old man."

The teenagers laugh. Kenny takes a drag from his cigarette and lines up his next shot.

"Eight ball in the side." And he banks the ball perfectly, ending the game. A few girls clap. "Nice shot," someone says. Kenny puts out his cigarette on the side of the pool table.

"Rack 'em."

"What happened next?" a guy asks.

"Nothing, man. But she left the next day. I was so pissed. I dropped so much coin on that chick, and all I got was a case of blue balls."

"Gotta pay to play," someone says.

"Oh dude, I love this part," Kenny says. He turns the pool cue upside down and holds it like a microphone. He sings and dances, puts his arm around Henry. "Sing it!" Kenny says, and they do:

> *"He's for the money, he's for the show*
> *Lido's a-waitin' for another go*
> *Lido, whoa-oh-oh-oh-oh..."*

* * * * *

The idea strikes while Henry is standing in the arts and crafts barn, surrounded by aisles of unpainted ceramic objects. He needs to earn Joann's affection; he will give her the dog she's always wanted.

It's more than he wanted to pay ($14 can buy 64 games of Pac-man), but it's perfect. And it will be worth it.

Henry takes his time, painting the entire dog

brown, the color of toasted marshmallows. Next, he paints the eyes and nose shiny black. While those are drying, he adds some metallic bronze rub to the dog's fur. But that doesn't look right, so he tries to wipe it off with a paper towel. And that just smears everything.

Crap.

Henry finds another jar of brown paint and starts over.

A few hours later, he emerges from the arts and crafts barn, victorious. She's going to love this dog, this gift from Henry. In his excitement, he runs down the dusty road, past the game-room, past the other campers and tents, all the way to the Martin family's camper. Joann is eating lunch at the picnic table, and Henry runs to her side, presenting the dog to her, with both hands, like a trophy.

"Hi! What's this?" Joann asks.

"Your puppy," Henry says, between pants of breath. "You said, you wanted, a puppy."

"Oh yeah! I totally forgot! How sweet!"

"I like the colors you chose," Mrs. Martin says. "So creative."

"Thanks," Henry says. "I painted it four times."

"Henry," Joann says, "I absolutely love it."

"No problem," says Henry, playing it cool, like Kenny would. "Just doing my job."

"It's so adorable," Joann says. "I'm going to call him Henry."

A knife, straight to the heart; his cheeks fill with blood again.

Joann pats the statue on its head. "Good little Henry. He's a good little boy."

Inside, Henry thinks, don't call it that. Please don't call it that. Call it anything in the world but that. Inside, that is what Henry thinks.

                    *   *   *   *   *

"Hot enough for ya?" His dad is asking him. But
Henry is drifting again, staring out at the brown
lake with its oval green island.

"Yeah," Henry says, "I guess so." Everyone is
here today, Martins included. Joann is laying out
on a blanket in front of Henry; her tan skin is
slathered in shiny, slippery baby oil; her white
bikini has strings on the sides, no bigger than
shoelaces.

Henry drifts far away, from Joann, from this
campground, from everything; he wishes he were
invisible.

And so, when the lifeguard blows his whistle,
frantically, it takes Henry a moment to react, to
understand what's going on. Soon, another
lifeguard blows her whistle, just as loud as the
first one. The two lifeguards are waving their
arms in the air. Some kind of signal.

"Everyone out of the water!" the first
lifeguard yells through a white cone.

"What's going on?" Joann asks.

"Someone's missing," Henry's dad says.

Crowds of people emerge from the murky brown
lake; Henry's mom and Mrs. Kowalski return to
their beach chairs; Robbie and Kenny are right
behind them; Robbie carries a mutilated wax-paper
Pepsi cup.

The bathhouse loudspeaker confirms what Henry's
dad said: "Would everyone please leave the water
immediately. This is not a safety break. I repeat,
this is not a safety break. Thank you."

When Robbie reaches Joann's towel, he dumps the
contents of his wax-paper cup on her, covering her
with sand.

"Robbie!" she shrieks. "You a-hole!"

"Aw, man," Kenny says. "That was cold."

"Dammit, Robbie," Robbie's mom says.

Joann stands and tries to wipe off the sand from her skin and hair; but it's no use. The sand sticks her oily skin like powdered sugar on a donut.

"You are such a jerk sometimes," Joann says to Robbie.

"You love it," Robbie says.

Joann shakes her head in disgust and marches off toward the bathhouse.

All the lifeguards are now lining up shoulder to shoulder in the shallow water; they join hands and begin to wade into deeper water together.

A human comb. They are dragging the lake.

Henry stands up, follows Joann from a distance to the bathhouse. Inside the men's room, he acts quickly, stacking two wooden benches atop one another; then he climbs up toward the opening; with one foot on top of a stall's partition, and one hand bracing the wall, Henry can see directly down into the women's showers.

And there she is.

But it is not Joann; immediately he knows, it is not Joann; it's the girl with only one leg. Kendra. She's huddled on a bench, crouched behind the door, as if she were hiding. And she's crying. Henry stares at her leg, at the stump, and before he can decide what to do next, the girl looks up at him, gives him the finger. Black mascara streams down her face. Henry is frozen. He doesn't know what to do. He wants to ask her what's wrong. And why is she hiding? Does she want to be invisible too? He wants to tell her that he understands--that things will be okay. That life's a bitch and then you die. Something. But before he can speak, Kendra begins removing her bikini top, one shoulder at a time, allowing Henry to watch. She undoes the clasp behind her back and the bikini top falls forward, revealing pale skin and brown nipples. Breasts. The first ones Henry has ever seen in person. Almost instantly, he feels the blood surging in his groin, and his hand wanders to find the source. Kendra continues to undress; she loops her thumbs inside the bikini bottom, and lifts herself off the bench, enough to slide the bikini over her stump; then she parts her legs, allowing Henry to look at her most private area--a triangle of black matted hair, and something is happening, deep within his loins. It starts in his stomach. Or maybe his toes. A tingling. Electricity. Surging through his body in waves; his knees buckle, his leg muscles go numb, his skin turns to pins-and-needles, and Henry is falling, falling, from his perch, grabbing at the air, and tumbling to the ground.

And just like that, it's over.

The world has stopped.

"Are you okay?" the girl is asking, from the other side of the wall.

"Yes," Henry says. "I'm okay." His elbow is bruised where he landed; his left shin is torn, bleeding; and his forehead will definitely have a lump. But in this moment, Henry feels no pain; so he sits on the floor and he waits for the bleeding to stop.

Outside, the commotion is over; the drama is gone; the lifeguards are no longer dragging the lake; they are instead huddled together, talking and laughing; whoever had gone missing must have been found, reunited with their family.

Henry retraces his steps, following the maze-like path back to his family and their blankets: left, right, up, right, up, right, right.

"What happened to you?" his mom is asking, staring at his forehead.

"What do you mean?" Henry replies.

"You're bleeding."

And then she is dabbing Henry's forehead with a blue t-shirt; she shows him a few drops of dark blood.

"What did you do!?"

"I'm not sure," he says.

His mom rummages through her beach-bag and hands Henry a compact mirror. He looks at the cut. A perfect ninety-degree angle. Like a number "7" on a digital clock.

"Cool," Henry says.

The loudspeaker announces that the beach is open again; kids and adults race back into the water, desperate to escape the heat and humidity.

Kenny taps Henry on the shoulder. "Hey boss, want to swim to the island?"

"Sure," Henry says, "Give me a minute."

Kenny takes off his mirrored sunglasses, hands them to Henry, who puts them on. He sits down on his towel and his body sinks into the earth, becomes connected to it. All around him is excitement, splashing, shrieks of laughter. But inside he is still and calm, a lake without waves. A poor man's reset. Henry doesn't even flinch when a bee lands on his knee-cap; he merely watches the bee, this strange, flying black-and-yellow insect, as it crawls in circles on his skin.

"Are you okay?" Joann is asking him.

"Yeah," Henry says. "Why wouldn't I be?" He doesn't look up at Joann; he just stares and stares at the bee on his skin, wondering what secrets it holds, what mysteries its body reveals. If he stares at the bee long enough, Henry thinks, he will figure out the pattern and the formula behind it. For such is the way the world works.

After a few moments the bee takes off, headed toward another family on another blanket. Henry stands and stretches, tossing the sunglasses onto

his towel. He looks out at the swimming lake,
searching for Kenny, and in the distance spots
him, doing handstands in water that is chest-deep.
So Henry walks toward the lake, across the grass,
around coolers and blankets, past the garbage cans
with their wasps, all the way to the sandy beach,
where kids build sandcastles only to wreck them
and build them again; Henry finds an open lane in
the sand and begins to run; he sprints into the
shallow water, half-galloping, until his shorts
are wet; then he closes his eyes and dives
headfirst; his hands touch sandy, mushy bottom,
and he kicks hard, propelling himself forward;
Henry swims and swims in the dark, heavy silence
of the lake. When his air runs out, he surfaces,
and the sounds come back to him, the splashing and
the screaming; he rubs his eyes, and the world too
returns, blue sky and white clouds, brown
shimmering water, and green, grassy island; Kenny
is there too, waving with both arms; Henry gives
him a thumbs-up, and with a deep breath, closes
his eyes and dives under once more.

A MORE REALISTIC YOU

Doreen sits in her car, a/c on high, ABBA Gold on repeat, while she waits for anyone else to show up. So far, it's just Doreen's Honda Civic and the chartered bus, stationed at opposite ends of the church parking lot, facing one another. Like an old-fashioned showdown, Doreen thinks. Because for maybe the tenth time today, she considers bailing out on this casino trip. If only she hadn't paid in advance, before all this business with Chaz (as he likes to be called now).

She rolls a cigarette between her fingers and lights it. Okay Doreen, here's the dealio: if no one shows up by the time this cigarette is finished, you can turn around and go straight home. Or drive to Charlie's (darn it, Chaz's!) and apologize; make amends with her son. Maybe even involve Shannon, his wife; surely she can help talk some sense into him.

Doreen cracks the window, then checks her reflection in the mirror. Lipstick looks good (Dusty Rose), mascara too, but today is one of those days, when she barely recognizes the person staring back at her. Or at least, the appearance of that person. The wrinkles. The loose skin. The thinning hair. A lifetime of worry and regret.

But still, Doreen doesn't *feel* sixty. The little voice inside her head, the one that dreams and thinks and laughs and cries, hasn't changed one bit. It's only the body that changes, Doreen thinks; the body ages, breaks down, and betrays that little voice inside our head.

Across the parking lot, the bus driver steps down from the bus and walks toward the church's side entrance; he's an older man, bowl-legged but surprisingly fast. He tries to open the side door, but finds it locked. Doreen knows from experience, that door is always locked.

When the man retreats toward the bus, Doreen cannot resist trying to help. She honks the horn and points to the church, mouthing the word "Front." But the man doesn't understand; he cups a hand to his ear and shrugs; then he stands there, waiting for Doreen to make the next move.

Well, I guess this is as good a sign as any, she thinks; the Lord works in mysterious ways. So Doreen turns off the ignition, puts out her cigarette, and gathers her purse.

*   *   *   *   *

All told, there are 32 people on this chartered bus from Parma Heights, Ohio, to Beckley, West Virginia. Some are new faces, but most are familiar to Doreen from Sunday services; the Vanderwahl's, the church's big donors are sitting up front; Peg and Darren Amstutz are here as well; Darren keeps standing up in the aisle; his tight bicycle shorts leave little to the imagination (Lordy, Lordy!); and of course, Bill Johnson is here too, the man who convinced Doreen to take this trip, over a few danishes on Palm Sunday.

"It'll be good for what ails you," he said. "Even if nothing's ailing you at all."

The first few hours of the trip are uneventful, just the drone of the bus's diesel engine and the occasional rattle of the huge windows in their panes; Doreen reads nearly sixty pages from the latest edition of "Chicken Soup for the Soul." But soon Doreen finds herself starting to eavesdrop on the conversation behind her; two young ladies are talking about getting pregnant.

"No way in hell," one of them says, "Could you convince me to have a baby."

"Tell me about it," the other woman says, her voice deeper, raspier. "It's like trying to shove a watermelon through a garden hose."

"Dakota said she was in labor for eighteen hours. That's like a whole day! Can you imagine?"

"I don't know. Maybe I'll feel differently someday. But for right now, having a baby seems like the dumbest idea in the whole world."

"Plus, I'll bet your husband won't have sex with you afterwards, 'cause you're all stretched out down there and stuff."

"Totally. Nothing good can come of it."

Doreen can't resist joining in; she folds her book shut and turns around, peeking her head up and over the seat.

"Hiyah, girls. Can I ask how old you are?"

"Twenty-four."

"Twenty-five."

"I couldn't help but overhear. Do you want to know the secret about babies?"

"What secret?" / "Sure."

From the way these two women are looking at her, Doreen guesses they are undecided whether she is a welcome distraction or a rude interruption.

"Okay," Doreen marches forward. "There's a love you feel for your parents, right? And a love you feel for your brothers and sisters. It's a different kind of love, but still... Then there's a love you feel for your friends. That's different too. And if you're lucky, there's a love you feel for your boyfriend, or your lover, whatever. And that feels like it's the most intense love you could ever know."

"Because of sex," says the girl with the raspy voice; her friend nods and offers up a reassuring high-five.

"Well, yes, in part," Doreen says. "But then you have a baby. And that too, is a different kind of love. But here's the dealio: the love you feel for your own son or a daughter is greater than all those other loves put together. Times a million."

"Hmmm," the girl with brown hair says, "Yeah, maybe."

Doreen winks and turns to face forward again. She is proud of herself; who knows, maybe she just made a difference in someone's life. Behind her, the girls whisper to one another again, then they both erupt in uncontrollable laughter.

Doreen stares out the window, lost in her own thoughts; the bus passes by a series of expansive cornfields. Rows upon rows of leafy green stalks pass by like an optical illusion, like cards being shuffled, or a series of memories hanging together by the smallest of threads.

She tries to nail down the exact moment their relationship began to erode. But right now all she can think about is Charlie as a teenager, fifteen years old, sleeping on the couch under an afghan while the television plays. Doreen turns off the TV and still he does not wake, so deep into sleep is this adolescent boy, this son of hers. So she tickles his feet, lightly, just like her own father used to do with her; but Charlie recoils at her touch, bucking violently; he kicks her hard in the thigh, shouting, "Stop it! I fucking hate it when you do that!" And Doreen tries not to appear hurt, so deeply wounded by this young boy in a man's body. And then days later, Doreen will find photocopied articles from medical journals scattered around the house, with sentences underlined and starred: "Tickling may cause anxiety, irritability, and even stuttering." But what will bother Doreen the most, is not the information itself, but rather how deeply the ink has been carved into the paper.

* * * * *

When the bus pulls into the casino parking lot, Doreen realizes she has made a mistake; she should not have come on this trip today; she should have stayed home and visited her estranged son, who has ceased answering her calls.

But before she can entertain any options to return home, Bill Johnson is standing before her, grinning like a mad man.

"Hey! You came!"

"Hi, Bill! Yes, I'm here. But I'm afraid I'm not feeling so well."

"Oh no... car sick?"

She nods, hoping it will be less of a lie.

"Well, we need to get you outside then. Get some fresh air." And he doesn't wait for a response; Bill Johnson takes her hand and escorts her to the front of the bus, down the steps, and out the door.

Outside, the sun blinds her briefly as she takes in the scene; an enormous royal palace painted orange and pink, adorned with neon lights of all colors. Blues and reds and yellows. Like a Christmas tree. Like nothing Doreen has ever seen.

"Wow," she says.

Bill Johnson, she realizes, is still holding her hand.

"Come on," he's saying. "Let's get you a club soda. Or some crackers. Something to settle your stomach."

The sign on the door says, "Welcome to Casino Palace. We're betting you'll have fun today!" Inside is a giant warehouse of activity, similar to what Doreen has seen on CSI: Las Vegas. But television did not, could not, prepare her for the complex assault on her ear drums: bells and whistles and beeping and boinking and blipping. Doreen freezes for a moment, staring at the mosaic carpet beneath her, a pattern similar to the stained-glass windows of her church; at any moment, Doreen imagines, the glass will break and send her tumbling straight to hell.

"What do you think?" Bill Johnson asks her.

"It's loud."

"You'll get used to it. Come on."

Bill Johnson escorts her to the bar, orders a club soda for Doreen, and a Manhattan for himself.

"I'm glad you came," he says. His breath hangs between them, like moth balls and fish oil.

"Thanks Bill," she says.

The casino is shaped like an octagon, Doreen realizes. In the center is a raised platform, almost like a stage, with blackjack and craps tables; all around the perimeter of the octagon are rows upon rows upon rows of slot machines and video poker; in the back are two cashier windows and the restrooms.

"Feel any better?" Bill asks.

"Yes, thank you," Doreen says.

"My wife used to get car sick all the time. Club soda and saltine crackers were the only things that would settle her stomach."

"Bill," she says.

"What?"

"Do you have any kids?"

"No. Why?"

"I was just curious."

"Oh."

Bill Johnson drains the rest of his Manhattan and orders another. Doreen has barely even touched her club soda.

"I'm glad you came today, Maureen," he says again, this time staring at her chest; and his breath surrounds them again, not unlike, Doreen thinks, a discrete passage of gas.

*   *   *   *   *

Hours later, and she still can't shake this man. They sit together, playing quarter slots. Bill Johnson is on his fourth or maybe fifth Manhattan, and Doreen is beginning to suspect him of stealing her tokens. For the umpteenth time, she scans the casino, searching for someone else from their church group, a distraction, a refuge, a savior.

"Can I borrow a token?" Bill Johnson asks, dipping his hand into her cup before she has a chance to answer.

"Sure," Doreen says.

His wrist brushes by her chest, and pauses there.

"S'cuse me," he says.

It's all she can take. Doreen gathers her purse and stands; she offers her cup of tokens to Bill Johnson.

"I need to use the restroom," Doreen says flatly. "Feel free to use these while I'm gone."

"Can you get me a drink?" Bill asks.

"Sure," Doreen says.

In the hallway outside the restrooms, Doreen

nearly collides with Peg and Darren Amstutz. But her enthusiasm quickly fades to embarrassment; the two are involved in a heated argument; Doreen hears Peg say "fucking the babysitter" before Darren puts a hand over Peg's mouth.

All the stalls are in use, so Doreen checks her appearance in the mirror; there's a swatch of lipstick on her teeth, and she wonders whether it's been there all day. Maybe that's what the girls behind her were laughing at on the bus. Who knows? When Doreen was younger, she thinks, that sort of thing would've bothered her. But not now. Every embarrassment hurts a little less now. Every heartache. Every death. And maybe that's how the little voice inside your head ages. It's still the same voice, just more realistic. Practical. More, she hates to admit, numb.

"Doreen?" someone is asking.

"Yes?"

"I'm Roxie."

Doreen turns to face her, but does not recognize the woman standing before her. Short, spiky gray hair. Pierced eyebrow. No makeup. Brown leather vest.

"Roxie Quinn, from Westlake High," she laughs easily. "You haven't changed a bit!"

"How are you?" Doreen asks, searching her memory banks, but she can't place the face. "It's been a long time."

"Oh, I'm okay, I guess. No complaints. Who would listen, right?"

"That's a good one."

Another stall door opens up, and it's Doreen's turn in line. She gestures toward the open stall.

"Welp, nature calls."

"Yah, of course. Hey, good luck out there, Doreen! Win some big money!"

"Thanks," Doreen says.

She steps into the open stall and latches the door, clutching her heavy purse against her chest. Then just as quickly, she unlatches the door and steps outside again; Roxie is just leaving the bathroom.

"Wait!" Doreen shouts, surprising herself with the intensity of her voice.

*   *   *   *   *

In less than fifteen minutes, Doreen learns: Roxie lives a mere two miles from her; neither of them moved away after high school. Roxie has three kids. The oldest works for a rental car agency; he gave her a free two-week rental for her 60th birthday. And so Roxie is on her way home from an unplanned and unmapped road trip: the Red River Gorge of Kentucky, Shenandoah National Park, Seneca Rock, the Cumberland Gap, Sherman's Cave, and "many places along the way."

Doreen can't help but ask: "So, what are the odds we'd run into each other here? When we both live in the same town? So weird."

"I would say the odds are one in two."

"One in two? I don't think so!"

"Well, either we were gonna meet up or we weren't. That's one in two."

"Hmm," Doreen says. "That's an interesting way to think about it."

"Play some craps?" Roxie asks.

"No, thank you. I don't know the first thing about it."

"Ah, come on. It's easy. Like shooting fish in a barrel." Roxie mimes shooting a rifle or shotgun. "Blam. Blam. Blam." Her spiked hair doesn't budge when she moves, Doreen notices. Doreen also likes the way Roxie's silver piercing catches the flashing lights of the casino, like a twinkle in the eye.

"Okay," Doreen says. "I'll try."

Roxie picks up Doreen's purse, hands it to her. "Jesus, what you got in this thing? Bowling balls?"

"Oh, I know. I need to clean it out. Throw some stuff away. Don't you carry a purse at all?"

"Nah," Roxie says. "Don't need one."

"Well, some stuff, you can't do without," Doreen says.

"Like what?"

"I don't know, stuff." Doreen unzips her purse, letting Roxie peer inside: wallet, book, makeup, gum, brush, receipts, aspirin, vitamins, comb, scarf, pencils, pens, scissors, band-aids, pads of paper, mints, coupons, prescriptions, Kleenex, and everything else. "Stuff!"

"Christ almighty, you got more junk in there than a pack-rat at a knick-knack convention. Tampons? When's last time you used a tampon?"

"Oh, they're not for me. They're just in case, I don't know, someone is in a bind. Or needs one. I guess they are getting pretty old."

"Ancient, is more like it. Some of them got cobwebs."

Doreen laughs. "Yeah, I know it sounds silly, but I like being prepared. I like being able to help people out when I can."

"Sounds like a sickness."

"Maybe it is," Doreen says. "But of all the sicknesses you can have, this one's not so bad!"

"As long as you don't put others' happiness before your own," Roxie says. "That's what martyrs do. And we all know where they end up."

"As angels," Doreen says.

"Nailed to a goddamn tree," says Roxie.

*   *   *   *   *

Years later, Charlie had shown up on Doreen's doorstep with Shannon in tow; both of them had been crying. At the time, they were newly engaged; Doreen can still remember the bright sparkling diamond on Shannon's finger; it was all Doreen could look at during the ensuing conversation, the confessions, the most awkward day of her life. According to Charlie, there had been infidelities on his part. Indiscretions, he kept calling them. But they were over with now. Charlie was getting help from a psychiatrist. Going to group therapy now. It's an addiction, Charlie said, to sexual intercourse. And he would need everyone's support. During all this, Shannon merely nodded, at Charlie, at Doreen; and for this, Doreen hated her. Doreen wanted to tell Shannon, run. And don't look back. He's just like his father. Run! But of course, she didn't say this. As a mother, she was required to show her acceptance and support. If this was what Charlie wanted, she would stand beside him. So she told him precisely that. "Thanks," Charlie said. "The doctor couldn't stress enough how important it was to get your support, knowing what he does about our relationship." Doreen stared at the diamond ring, wondering how much it cost, probably a lot, more than she'll ever know, because Shannon just kept nodding, nodding, nodding.

"Don't worry about all those boxes and words," Roxie was saying. "For now, just focus on that white puck right there." But Doreen could barely follow Roxie's words, "..the shooter, the come-out roll, the pass line bet, making the point.."

"And whatever you do," Roxie says, "Don't bet on anything that sounds cool. Like snake eyes or boxcars."

"Can you just tell me," Doreen says, "When it's my turn."

Roxie laughs, and Doreen watches the dealer collect chips, stack chips, and push chips toward the bettors; Doreen stares at the green felt table with the confusing boxes and words; and just like that, Roxie is handing her the dice.

"Lady luck," Roxie says. "Let's see what you got, Reenie."

Doreen shuts her eyes and tosses both dice.

"Winner!"

*　　*　　*　　*　　*

Afterwards, they shuffle to the bar together. The casino is more crowded now; people bump into other people, excuse themselves past one another. The place is so crowded, Doreen can no longer discern the shape of the casino, the octagon; even the mosaic floor tiles have disappeared beneath a stampede of legs and feet.

"Well, that sure was a hoot," Roxie says. "I'd buy you a drink, but it looks like you're the big moneybags today."

"Beginner's luck," Doreen says.

"Then how'd you know to triple the bet when the point was ten?"

"You're a good teacher, I guess," Doreen says. "And besides, ten is my lucky number. I was born on 10/10/58. At ten o'clock too!"

"Well, crap on a cracker!"

Seated nearby, with his head on the bar, is Bill Johnson. When Doreen and Roxie approach, the man stirs, picks his head up.

"Time's it?"

"Almost four," says Doreen. And Bill Johnson resumes his snooze on the bar.

"You know that guy?" Roxie asks.

"Sort of. He's part of our church group. He kind of invited me today."

"Sorry to hear that," says Roxie. Then, "Hey, you're not married are you? I don't see a ring."

"Divorced. But I'm not... you know..."

"What? A lesbian?"

"Yes. Thank you." Doreen blushes.

"Don't worry, I'm not hitting on you, Darling! Besides, no such thing as a lesbian. People fall in love with people, not sex organs. Just so happens, women usually have more about them to love."

Doreen lights a cigarette, glances at Bill Johnson. "Now that, I can agree with."

"But I wonder," Roxie says. "How your church group would feel about that."

"Probably not good," she laughs, suddenly embarrassed. She wants to tell Roxie that she is more open-minded than them. That she agrees with the overall structure of the church, but not all of its teachings. That she would vote in favor of gay marriage, if it ever comes up on the Ohio ballot. But instead, she blurts out: "My son won't let me see my grandchild."

"Beg your pardon?"

"My son," Doreen pauses, exhales some smoke. "He won't let me see my grandbaby."

"How come?"

"He says I'm dangerous around her."

"You? Dangerous?" Roxie laughs. "I'm sorry, Doreen. Not trying to make light of things. It's just, you're the last person in the world that comes to mind when I think about dangerous."

"I don't make good decisions, I guess."

"Get in line."

"No, I mean, I don't *think* about things. That's what Charlie says. Or Chaz. My son wants to be called Chaz now."

"And what, was Chaz referring to when he said that?"

In Doreen's mind, two stories begin to converge and overlap; in one version, the baby is Hayden, Charlie's daughter and her grandchild; in another version, the baby is Charlie, her own son. So many years ago.

"I gave the baby a gummy bear."

"A gummy bear? One of them little candies?"

"Yes. A red gummy bear. It got stuck in her throat and she almost choked."

"Sounds like an accident to me."

"That's what I said. But Charlie doesn't believe in accidents. He says everything happens for a reason."

"Aw, horse-puckey. That's just how our noggins work. Shit happens then we give it a reason. It's how we make sense of things, I guess."

"Hmmm," Doreen says.

"Give you an example," Roxie says, "What's the reason you and I met up down here, even though we live only a few miles apart?"

"I don't know."

"Exactly. But one day you will. It's how our noggins work. I guaran-fuckin-tee it."

*   *   *   *   *

At 6:00 p.m., it's time to go home. Roxie and Doreen walk together outside. The transition is blinding. It seems so bright, compared to the crowded darkness of the casino. Nearby the charter bus is parked in a fire lane, idling; the bowl-legged man is standing by the curb with a clipboard.

"Well, my car is over there," Roxie says. "What are you going to do?"

"I think I should take the bus. With my church group."

"No, silly. I mean about your son."

"Oh, I don't know yet. I guess I need some time to think about that one."

"Just remember, if you don't like the reason, it's not too late to change it."

"I will. Thanks. It was really, well, refreshing to meet you."

"Right back atcha, Reenie. Look me up if you ever want to raise some heck together."

"I will," Doreen says.

They hug, and Doreen watches Roxie saunter toward the parking lot; Doreen can't help but admire the woman's confident gait. Before she steps aboard the charter bus, Doreen pauses at a garbage can and opens her purse.

"Don't need you anymore," she says, throwing away the tampons. "Or your cobwebs."

Soon, they are traveling again, but the mood is different now. Complacent. Almost sedated. Bill Johnson snores; the two girls who sat behind Doreen are now seated in separate rows, also trying to sleep; the Vanderwahl's sit beside one another in silence; the Amstutz's have entirely disappeared; Doreen wonders how they got home.

Before long, the bus crosses over the Ohio River and the farmlands begin again, the rolling hills, and the immense cornfields with their hypnotizing symmetrical rows.

Charlie is barely eleven months old, and Doreen has just finished changing his diaper. She opens the baby powder and dusts his legs and feet, rubbing them gently, and Charlie giggles. It makes Doreen giggle too. So she does it again, a few times, before she decides to take a picture, so she'll remember this moment forever. She carries Charlie with her to the bedroom for the camera, and the two of them return to the baby's room. Doreen sets baby Charlie on the changing table and looks through the tiny viewfinder; and in the

split second that follows: Charlie bucks with his
legs, just enough to send his body flipping off
the changing table. Doreen can see it happening,
but can't move fast enough to catch him. Charlie
lands on his head, his neck bending grotesquely,
his body following. But it's the sound of his soft
head hitting the hardwood floor that stays with
her. It keeps playing over and over in her mind,
long after he screams and cries; long after they
have left the hospital, and the emergency room;
long after Charlie has grown up, and married, and
had a child of his own. The sound is here with her
now, and she prays, she prays, she prays to God
that one day she will be worthy, and that sound
will finally disappear.

REPORT # 0673543
[Translated from the Cerulean
by J.C. Lagowski]

"My recommendation for Planet #0673543 [aka
Earth]," Kevin033 wrote in his report, "is
complete and total annihilation." He paused to
consider the options--solar event, planetary
virus, military invasion--before realizing that
his larger pincer was indeed shaking. Perhaps it
was stress; he couldn't remember the last time
he'd had a decent hibernation period; or perhaps
it was some sort of cognitive dissonance, for
Kevin033 was not unaware of the irony of the
situation. Because this, his final report after
6,720 years, was about to become his first and
only recommendation for destruction. In the past,
the other agents had teased him, saying he was too
klepfotch, but in every case, Kevin033 had been
able to identify a Murphy01 Event, a signal of
progress, a glimmer of hope. And this, more than
anything, he credited for his impressive ranking
amongst the Kevins.
   Outside his office window, the atmospheric
gases were beginning their nightly dances,
flashing in darker hues of purple and orange and
green, becoming thicker and slower with each
pulse. The magnetic season was almost here.

And yet still, something about this recommendation was troubling him. Twice he had delayed the termination of the non-locality pairings; even now three signals were still open, one of them attached to his own neural scout, JCL01. Kevin033 wanted to be certain, but not absolute, in true Cerulean fashion. For this scouting report, the longest and most exhaustive of his career, was sure to carry him upwards, perhaps all the way to Kevin10 status, a seat among the Elder's Council. And so he was eager to finish the 168-year project, eager to put aside the stress of work and savor the enviable life of a retired Cerulean. Play some bogdorf. Relax in the Sea of Arsenic. Just as his own father, Carl212, had done. And his father before him, Larry071.

"What's up, Kevin-billion?" joked Barney89, poking his head into the office. "You still working on #0673543?"

"Almost finished."

"From what I've heard, it's a real transport-wreck."

"Just want to be sure," said Kevin033.

"Still looking for a Murphy01?"

Kevin033 shrugged.

"You won't find it. Besides, if it makes you feel any better, those organics are already destroying their ecosystem. All we'd be doing is speeding it up."

"Thanks."

"Hey, when you're done, can you stop by the Transition Room? I'd like to show you something."

Kevin033 nodded, returning to his evaluation; there was no doubt he'd been thorough, extremely thorough. Overly-generous, Alison40 would say. Why then the uncertainty?

As indicated in the findings section, Kevin033

wrote, the main problem with Planet #0673543 appears to be symmetrical. There is a critical lack of trilateral symmetry in both organic and inorganic structures. And here, he paused, remembering his favorite exception to this generalization, the earth fruit called the banana. How he loved the taste of this fruit! It was his sole indulgence during all the years spent inside the anxiety-filled brain of CJL01.

And for a moment, Kevin033 re-visited the neural activity associated with his research; some days, his scout [CJL01] would create lively, fictitious scenarios with plastic replicas of organic creatures [What were their names again? Walrus-man? Hammer-tooth? His favorite was Greedo]; other days they would eat delicious bananas and listen to synthetic vibrations from a file source known as "Metallica." But mostly, CJL01 just stayed in bed; his physical appearance, Kevin033 knew, had been altered by a tragic experience; many years ago, his neural scout had nearly been burned alive in a fire.

Back in the office of his own planet, Kevin033 continued his report. The intelligent organic beings display mostly bilateral symmetry [with noted exceptions in the plant and aquatic groups, where radial symmetry appears on a lesser scale]. Apparently, a genetic fluke or inactive protein prevented this planet's asymmetrical creatures [sponges] from developing a central nervous system, and thus evolving into intelligent asymmetric organics. Whatever the cause of that fluke, Kevin033 wrote, its consequences have been positively disastrous.

From a biological perspective, this bilateral structure promotes cephalization, where nervous tissue concentrates toward one end of a stem, producing a head and/or sensory organs [n.b.

compare to the radial structures found in 003778 and 019993]. The result is a brain organ atop a spinal column with unchecked growth potential. In particular, the dominant species [human organics] studied on #0673543 show a disproportionately large cerebral cortex, notably in the frontal lobes. Most alarming is the enormous dorsal lateral prefrontal cortex [DLPC], which governs many critical areas of cognition, including planning, inhibition, and evaluation.

Coupled with the neurotransmitter dopamine, this has the following effects on cognitive processing: 1. A binary storage/retrieval system; objects are coded and stored by "either/or" not "both"; this leads to a polarization of concepts and undue segmentation; 2. Excessive pattern construction and causality inference; the organics find links where there are none; they attribute supernatural forces to everyday objects and occasions, 3. Self-gratification; there is a distinct and measurable experience of pleasure [dopamine rush] associated with both statements above, regardless of objective truth.

In conclusion, the errant symmetries of Planet #0673543 have resulted in a dominant, self-congratulatory, absolutist group of organics which further divides [and subdivides] itself according to irreconcilable supernatural belief systems.

"It is," as one agent reported, "A hot mess."

Recommendation: Destruction by cosmic event.

What more is there to say after that? If the Council of Elders challenged his recommendation, Kevin033 had reams and reams of data to back up his conclusion. And after all this time, the elders would not question his judgment. The recommendations would be carried out over the next few weeks [or in about two hours on Earth].

And so Kevin033 felt only the slightest

hesitation as he disconnected the remaining neural pairings, solidified the report, and published his findings to the Elders. Soon it would all be over, for #0673543--and for his long and unblemished career. Kevin033 had imagined this day for so long, he was not sure how to feel. He closed his larger eye and reached for his portable nitrogen inhaler; this de-ionized office atmosphere always made his alveoli flare up. From down the hallway, pleasant vibrations were emanating; the rhythm sounded northern, upbeat, celebratory. The Transition Room? He decided to find out.

The door was closed, but Kevin033 could hear many Ceruleans exchanging signals inside; and the rhythmic vibrations were loud enough to signal a celebration of some kind. A promotion? A life event? A quelstark?

He opened the door and was greeted by familiar faces. "Surprise!" they said. The gathering was for him! Of course, a transition party for his upcoming retirement. His co-workers were all here, friends and family too! Three of his wives were seated at the table, along with his offspring; even his mating partner Alison40 had been invited. She smiled at him; he smiled back, noting how unevenly her warped body fit inside her garments.

Tears came to his smaller eye. "I had no idea," Kevin033 said.

"Ha ha!" said Barney89. "We gotcha! One week early my good friend!"

On the table was his favorite Cerulean indulgence: fermented nectar cake--and in the shape of an Earth sponge! What a funny joke! In addition, there were quantum bursts of colored magnetism orbiting above their heads, and covered packages for him to unwrap and take ownership. Kevin033 was overwhelmed; he sat in the primary chair and placed his offspring upon one of his laps. Gary545 greeted him with a hug.

"Can I open your covered boxes?" Gary545 asked, drooling slightly.

"We can do it together," Kevin033 responded. "Little Five-four-five."

And together they tore through the outer wrappings of the boxes, revealing books and optical devices and bottles of fermented plant juice, letters of congratulations and wishes for a happy, healthy retirement.

"This will be one of my 100 favorite memories," Kevin033 told them. "Out of the millions I have already." And he meant it.

Later, when he was alone with Alison40, he asked her if she had known about the party that had surprised him so. Yes, she confessed, it had been her idea. Then she purred softly, laying back among the hibernation pillows. "Allow me then," Kevin033 said, "to thank you properly." The two embraced and began the intricate rituals of Cerulean mating; both of them began vibrating softly, slowly at first; his reproductive organ began changing color and dilating for osmosis; she relaxed, pushing aside her genital feathers, allowing him access to her ova storage. But then, without warning, Kevin033 sat up with great alarm.

"A banana!" he exclaimed.

"What banana?" Alison40 demanded.

"There's a banana." He gasped, reaching for his nitrogen inhaler.

"What nonsense are you talking about?"

He took three deep nitrogen blasts before he spoke. "Right now, JCL01 is eating a banana. I'm sure of it."

"How can that be? You said you disconnected the neural pairings."

"I did. I did stop the pairings. But I can taste it now. As sure as we're sitting here. He's eating a banana."

"Kevin033, this is highly unusual.

"I'm sorry," he said. "This has never happened before. Maybe I missed something."

"I know you," Alison40 said. "And you never miss anything. It's why you'll be a Kevin10 soon, sitting at the Council of Elders."

She stroked the hibernation fur on the back of his ear stalk. But Kevin033 was in a daze, lost in dreams without sleep. He envisioned JCL01 sitting on the steps outside his dwelling, looking up at a clear night sky, eating a perfectly ripe banana. The image was so strong, Kevin033 could taste the fruit, see the twinkling stars, and feel the paralyzing anxiety of CJL01. It was almost as though the two organisms had fused into one.

Kevin033 looked down; on his small and singular lap was the slightest of objects, a paper envelope containing a message; it was an invitation of some sort, a call to action or duty. Kevin033 tried to make out the words, the letters, but it was impossible; the image was already disappearing. And just like that, Kevin033 returned to the hibernation chamber with Alison40.

"I think," said Kevin033, "I may have overlooked something."

"You're being too hard on yourself. Please, lover, come back to me."

"The Murphy01 Event. I couldn't see it because I was standing too close."

"What are you saying?"

"The Murphy01 Event. It's happening right now."

"I don't follow."

"The Murphy01. It's my scout."

THE VIOLENCE OF MEN

V. hates everything about this discount store.
Its narrow, crowded aisles, its shitty off-brand
selections, and especially, Jesus Christ,
especially the workers in their orange vests who
move at the speed of tree sap. He hates that he
must drive Etta to this place, her palsy making it
impossible to operate a vehicle (or sign a check
for that matter). And he hates himself right now,
for forgetting to eat breakfast this morning; two
cups of coffee moving straight through him. His
medications, also forgotten, are still sitting in
the Tuesday compartment of the seven-day reminder
system, which itself is sitting on the window
ledge above the kitchen sink.

"What does this price say?" Etta is asking him.

"How the hell should I know?" She can't hold
the cantaloupe steady, and he can't read the tiny
numbers on the white tag.

He wrests the cantaloupe from her hand.

"We need this," he says, setting the ball of
fruit carefully in the cart's empty child seat.

"I like to know how much we're spending."

"Two bucks."

"You didn't even look."

V. pushes the cart forward. "Come on," he says. "I'd like to get out of here before I'm dead." But one of the cart's rear wheels is stuck; it scuffs and slides on the dusty floor. V. gives it a good kick and it un-sticks for a moment. Then sticks again.

"Goddammit," he says.

"Do we need iceberg lettuce?" Etta asks, her head bobbing ever so slightly.

Too many questions; he pushes the cart and its stuck wheel forward, out of the produce aisle and toward the hardware section. His knuckles are fat and sore with arthritis, olive skin and unruly veins.

"Where are you going?" Etta asks, shuffling to keep up. "I have a list."

"Let me see that list," V. says, turning. The handwriting is frenetic, smudged. But she has written in large enough loops for V. to make out the words. "No, no, no, and no," he says. "We're not buying shaving cream here. Too expensive."

"But you're all out."

"No, I'm not. Just get your spices."

"I saw the can in the garbage."

"You're imagining things."

"And you're a grouch."

"Ah," V. says, turning away from her again; and suddenly the urge to pee is upon him. He can't remember if he's gone yet today; he thinks he recalls a few grateful squirts of pee in the shower; but that might have been yesterday.

"Hurry up," he tells her. And she disappears again.

From the shelf he grabs a can of WD-40 and un-tapes the thin red straw; squinting, V. is able to insert the straw's tip into the aerosol cap. He shakes the can and sprays the bad wheel liberally.

Lubricant bubbles and foams, dripping onto the floor. He lifts the cart and punches down on the wheel, freeing it from the axle.

Success.

The lubricant's smell reminds him of the plant. And how much he misses it. The organization of the maintenance shed, every part and tool in its place. The half-moons of grease under his fingernails. The endless repairs to the storage tanks, the pipelines, the boilers, tow motors, pumps, and timers. But more than anything, he misses the busy-work, the occupation of it all. The complete and utter absorption of his mind to the task at hand.

Etta returns with four spice jars: garlic salt, garlic powder, onion salt, and onion powder. She must be making stuffed cabbage again.

V. lifts the shopping cart slightly, kicks the wheel with his toe, to show Etta his handy-work. "Not bad for an old grouch."

"What? What's not bad?"

"I fixed the wheel."

"You got the floor all wet," Etta says, dumping the spices into the cart.

She's right, of course. A decent puddle of grease has settled on the worn linoleum; and a few shoppers are headed their way, a woman with three kids, and behind them, an enormous fellow on a three-wheeled scooter.

"You know what?" V. says, but never finishes his thought. Instead, he snatches a roll of paper towels from the shelf and tears into it.

"Don't open that," Etta says.

V. wipes up the spill and stands. Etta is frowning.

"Now we have to pay for those."

"Don't worry about it," he says. V. stretches and places the paper towels on the top shelf, making sure they are out of her reach.

"They have cameras here, you know," Etta says, her cheeks flushing.

"If you need me," V. says, "I'll be outside."

* * * * *

His fingers still smell like lubricant, and V. wipes them on his pants.

The man got what he deserved, V. tells himself again, hoping that with repetition and over time he will believe it. But it's been thirteen years now, and things haven't changed one bit. V. still has a choice whether or not to strike his boss, Don Waterson, with a 15" crescent wrench; and still he opts to swing, breaking the man's jaw in two places and shattering three teeth.

Someone had to do something, V. thinks. A man nearly lost his life, and it had been Don's fault. At least, he's pretty sure it was. The logbook had been altered, that's a fact; V.'s own handwriting had been over-written, scratched out; and who else but Don would do that? Trying to save a few bucks no doubt. Because for whatever reason, V.'s instruction to the second shift: "Purge line 765b with N2 gas" had been shortened to "Purge line 765b"; and so the second shift had merely flushed the pipe with soap and water; the residual moisture corroded the pipe, causing it to burst while Larry fastened the coupling to a tanker car; the blast of chlorine nearly killed him.

V. was the first one to respond; Larry on the ground next to the tanker car, the yellow/green gas still billowing from the pipe; V. recalls the smell, like bleach and pepper spray, as he dragged Larry away from the burst pipeline. The man's eyes were already swollen and watering; he gasped for air, but none would come; so V. rolled the man onto his side and tugged at his collar.

"Tell my wife..." Larry says, but V. doesn't let him finish.

"I'm not your damn messenger. Tell her yourself." Then V. leaves him, running off to find an oxygen tank and call an ambulance. He knows he doesn't have much time; from the Army, he knows what chlorine does to the body; the military used it before mustard gas; it turns to hydrochloric acid in your lungs, dissolving membranes, drowning you in your own fluids.

V. will not let Larry die like this.

He runs and runs, over railroad ties, and gravel, and onto the plant's greasy concrete floor. V. runs and runs, his legs never tiring, his eyes never losing focus.

And then, years later, after Larry has made a full recovery, V. will have dreams where he doesn't strike Don with the wrench, where V. is not forced into early retirement, and in fact, dreams where Larry himself admits to altering the log book; a simple misunderstanding. But these are just dreams, V. tells himself; false memories haunting a stubborn old man.

* * * * *

The parking lot of the discount store is filled with cars, V. notices, and morons. It's the price one pays, he thinks, for shopping in the morning on a Tuesday. The only people out here right now are old farts and unemployed losers.

He wonders which he is.

Next door is a Subway restaurant, and V. wanders to the door. He needs to find a bathroom soon; his bladder is full and cramping. But the door is locked.

Why didn't he go before they left? There had

been a good fifteen minutes of waiting on Etta
while she putzed around, rifling through the junk
drawer, clipping coupons, and feeding the cat, all
while she made out her list. "Multi-tasking" she
calls it. "Scatter-braining," he calls it.

For a moment V. considers driving to a gas
station or a Mcdonald's, but Etta would panic when
she sees the car missing. He decides to go back
inside the discount store.

He steps on the entrance pad, but the automatic
door does not open. Someone's fat kid is standing
on the other side of the door, putting weight on
the pressure-sensitive pad. V. motions for him to
back up, but the kid just stares at him,
curiously.

"Move back!" V. yells. But no response. Soon
another kid, a chubby little girl, joins the boy
in gazing up at this strange old man, yelling at
them from the other side of the glass door. They
giggle.

Move it, you runts, V. thinks. I've got to take
a piss!

V. bangs on the glass, trying to get someone's
attention. This scares the kids; they run off
toward their mother.

And finally the door opens.

Jesus.

The open registers have long lines and the
closed ones are blocked by chains. V. must go
around them, past the giant clearance bins, and
past the produce section once again, before
reaching the center of the store.

Another thing he hates about this place--it
feels like they are herding people through a maze
like fucking cattle.

He spots Etta waving to him from the longest
checkout line.

"Where'd you go?" she asks, chin bobbing.

"Looking for a bathroom."

"I need you to hold my place for a minute."

"Why?"

"I forgot the iceberg lettuce. Please?"

He sighs. "Hurry up."

While she is gone, V. takes advantage to move the cart to a shorter checkout line. Only four people ahead of him now. But the cashier has long nails, nearly two inches long, he estimates, and she seems intent on not breaking them while she keys in the prices. It's beyond frustrating. It's infuriating. And he's about to wet his pants.

Fuck sake.

"Why don't they open another line?" he says out loud, to anyone who will listen. The other shoppers ignore him or shrug. Crazy old man.

Someone pushes a cart behind V., and bumps into V.'s ankle, striking him squarely on the Achilles tendon.

"Oops," the man says. "Sorry."

"Watch it!" V. says, lifting his foot off the floor, rubbing the tendon.

The man scowls back and shrugs. "It was an accident." This guy is younger, 35 or 40, with small arms and a big stomach; and he refuses to break eye contact with V.

"What?" this man says. "What do you want me to do about it?"

The blood rushes to V.'s face, hot and invigorating. His hands become fists. And it's upon him once again. That old feeling. Like a switch in the brain. V. exhales and breaks eye contact, looking for Etta.

"That's what I thought," the other man says.

V. clenches his teeth and turns to face the checkout line in front of him. Violence has been a part of his life for as long as he can remember. His father taught him how to fight, how to make a

fist so you don't break your thumb. He recalls the
first time; or what he thinks was the first time.
V. and his brother Andy had run home from a
neighbor's house. One of the kids there had shot
Andy in the leg with a BB-gun; and there was a
welt on his skin to prove it. V.'s father had
said, "What the hell are you doing here for? Go
back there and kick his ass!" And so they had,
running all the way over to the neighbor's house,
bursting through the screen door, and chasing the
boy upstairs to his own room, where they sat on
top of him, punching him and kicking him. The boy
laid on his stomach, covering his head in defense.
So V. twisted the boy's arm behind his back, and
in his adrenaline-rushed state, pushed a little
too hard. The arm made a sickening crack, like a
tree branch, and the boy screamed. V. and Andy ran
out of there, down the stairs, past the boy's mom,
out the front door and back home. It was only when
they reached the comfort and safety of their own
house, that V. realized he was crying.

Afterward, there had been many fights. It
seemed like someone was always challenging him, or
humiliating him in some way. At school, they
called him "Big Ears" or "Big Nose." In the Army,
it was "Wop" and "Dago." But he always stood up to
the challenge, in the boxing ring, or behind a bar
on a Saturday night. But never, never in front of
Etta; he won't let her see him that way.

And so he forces a smile when she returns.

"Oh, there you are," she says. "Why did you
switch lines?"

"Nevermind," he says. A quick glance at the
other checkout line reveals what he suspects: it's
moving twice as fast as this line.

V. leans over to see what the holdup is. Two
people in front of him, an old woman is counting
out change from her coin purse. The cashier also

counts it, one fingernail ticking down on each and every coin.

Each. And. Every. Coin.

"Do they have a bathroom here?" V. asks Etta.

Before she can answer, a cashier appears next to them, unhooking the chain and opening a new checkout line.

"Are you opening?" the man behind V. asks.

"I'll take whoever's next," the cashier says, retreating to her register.

"Thank God," V. says, pulling back on the cart's handle, spinning toward the open line.

But the man behind V. has the same idea. He launches his own cart forward, trying to cut in front of V. and Etta.

V. grabs the front of the man's cart, halting it, while pushing his own cart into the open lane.

"Let go!" the man says. "Asshole!"

"We were first," V. says firmly, his cheeks flushing again.

"I asked her if she was open," the man says.

"Sorry," Etta says to the man. "We're sorry."

"We were here first," V. says again. "End of story."

The man does not respond, but instead begins ramming his cart into V.'s ankles again. Twice. Then three times. V. turns to stop the cart with his hand, but not before the cart strikes Etta in the hip.

"Ow," she says.

Or at least, that is what V. thinks she says. That is how he'll remember it. Because he can no longer hear her. Or the beeping of the scanners, or the clicking of the registers. The world has gone silent. V. shoves the man's cart again, firmly, spinning it out of his way; and inside V.'s head a pattern emerges--his footwork, the combinations, the angles. He will step in with his left foot, throwing a left jab high and to the man's right; the man will step to his left to avoid the jab, then V. will step into the next punch, torquing his body for power, and strike the man squarely on the nose, shattering the bone.

The space between the two men is scarcely six feet now; but it takes forever to cover the distance. The man is poised, scowling, waving his hands to call V. forward; other shoppers gasp and stare; surrounding them are colorful displays of chips and batteries and lighters and candy; these are the details that burrow into V.'s brain in this moment; they are what he will remember in years to come; but right now, someone else is controlling V.'s body, executing his plans; right now he has been reduced to a memory, of a boy running down the sidewalk, running as fast as he can, his lungs burning, his eyes watering, but still, running and running and running, toward a house. It's either the neighbor's or his own. Right now, it's impossible to tell. He just runs and runs and runs.

JULIE'S FIRST DAY!

Deja vu strikes Julie as she is reviewing paperwork with the woman named Mary Ann. Something about the phrase "401k" triggers it; Julie imagines she's been here before, starting this same job, sitting at this same table with this woman named Mary Ann. And just when she's about to shake it off, the feeling echoes again, peaking when Julie says, "No thanks, I'll take the cash!"

Mary Ann laughs, "Reminds me of myself when I was your age." She's kind and large and smells like lavender; Mary Ann slides a pen across the table to Julie. "Okay, this next one is a tax form."

But it's too late; Julie is now buzzing with anxiety or curiosity over the deja vu; she thinks about mentioning this to Mary Ann, then just as quickly, changes her mind.

"Do you mind if I use the restroom?" Julie asks, noting how her inflection rises at the end of sentences.

"Sure. The key is on the hook over there," Mary Ann says, pointing.

The women's bathroom is clean and brightly lit.

Julie stares at her reflection for a moment, evaluating the new apron and nametag, then decides to record this moment in her personal history. She snaps three quick pics on her phone.

Julie Coleman, working at Starbucks; her friends will crack up!

She sorts through the images, deleting the first one immediately (eyes are half-closed, looks like she's on drugs); the second one positively highlights her new zit (delete delete delete); the third one is halfway decent; good smile; good hair; she uploads it to Facebook.

Caption: "Julie's first day!"

It's not easy making a green apron look totally hot, Julie thinks; but maybe, just maybe, she pulled it off today with her skinny jeans, Hollister top, and chestnut Uggs. Julie smiles when she notices the Sillybandz still tangled around her wrist; last night at the dinner table Carrie assigned her these three, explaining each one in blissful ten-year-old detail: a yellow sunshine (Julie's always positive!), a pink dolphin (Julie loves animals!), and a blue question mark (Julie is a mystery!). Julie knows these gimmicks are $5 a pack and wonders how many packs her parents must have bought for Carrie, the spoiled little brat.

The new pic appears on her profile page, so Julie scrolls through her updates for the third time this morning. Still no word from Josh. Maybe the deja vu was an omen, a sign that they are breaking up for good this time.

She wants to believe the strange feeling means something, even if that something is very bad; she's so tired of people telling her what to believe and what not to believe.

Lies, lies, lies.

She sees that Josh posted a video last night.

So she clicks "like," just to remind him that she's out here, waiting.

Then she untangles the Sillybandz from her wrist and flushes two of them down the toilet; the blue question mark she keeps, winding it twice around her thumb; a reminder not to call or text Josh, until he calls her.

Be a mystery, Julie!

Then with a paper towel, she opens the door latch and returns to the table with Mary Ann.

"All set?" asks the larger woman.

"All set."

"Okay, let's review the ordering system again."

"Sounds good," says Julie, sitting down in a metal chair; but instead she surveys her new surroundings. Everything here is brown or tan or green; it is a Starbucks like any other Starbucks she has ever seen, with one small difference: on the back wall are taped dozens of children's drawings ("hand-turkeys" she remembers), tracings of tiny hands, colored with bright crayons to create Thanksgiving turkeys. Some of them have pilgrim hats or those gross, saggy red things hanging from their necks (what are they called again?); but Julie is most interested by a small misshapen turkey hanging near the bottom of the collection. The bird is colored in shiny black crayon, scribbled with great fury. She wonders whose kid this is or what he was thinking when he chose that crayon, colored that turkey.

*   *   *   *   *

They had been making out for nearly an hour, on the couch in Josh's basement, his parents still in Florida. The movie had long since ended, and the DVD player had returned to the menu screen, the theme music to "Eclipse" playing over and over and

over while they kissed. Josh had managed to
unclasp her bra, and push her sweater up, when his
hand abruptly slid down the front of her jeans.

"Whoa," Julie had said, grabbing his wrist.
"Where do you think you're going?" She had
intended it to sound sexy, playful; but instead,
to her shock and horror, it came out sounding like
her mom.

Josh locked eyes with her. "Well if I'm not
going down there, I'm going to bed."

"Josh!"

"What? Julie! How long have we been going out?"

"I was only kidding. Calm down."

"The hell you were. It's the same thing every
time. I'm sick of it."

"Josh, I didn't say you couldn't. I just wanted
you to, I don't know, slow down a little or
something." And maybe it was the angry look on his
face, or her lack of sleep the past few nights,
but for whatever reason, tears began welling up in
her eyes.

"Oh, Jesus Christ," Josh had said, standing to
adjust the bulge in his khaki pants. "You're
driving me crazy, Jules! You have no idea what
this is like!" His voice cracked, and if it
weren't for the intensity of the situation,
would've made her laugh.

"I'm sorry," she had said, suddenly feeling
naked, exposed; her breasts were still wet with
Josh's saliva; she dried them with her sweater and
re-clasped her bra.

"This is bullshit," Josh said; then he stomped
to the bathroom and slammed the door. Julie wasn't
sure what was going to happen next; she'd never
seen him so angry; so she grabbed her purse and
ran out the front door.

At home, the house was completely dark, a good
sign; Mom must be in bed. Julie was done crying

now and took her time not to make the slightest noise while opening the side door.

When she reached the stairs to the second floor, she took off her shoes and crept on the outermost edges of the steps, holding the walls for balance; from experience, she knew which steps would creak the most and avoided them altogether.

Finally, reaching the safety of her bedroom, Julie closed the door and turned on a light. But her cover had been blown.

The bed was stripped; the pillows she had strategically placed under the covers were now on the floor; even the princess wig now lay in a sad little heap near the trash-can.

Shit.

Before she could even think about what to do next, her door swung open.

Mom.

In her robe.

Arms crossed.

"Where have you been?" she asked.

"At Josh's."

"Oh, Julie." Rolling her eyes.

"Oh Julie, what?"

"Were his parents home? What were you thinking, sneaking out like this on a school night?"

"I don't know. I guess I wasn't."

"It's three in the morning! And did you forget, the SATs are in two days."

"So?"

"So?! Julie, you're in big trouble here. We'll talk about this tomorrow."

"What? Mom!?! They said you could take that test as many times as you want."

"We'll talk about it tomorrow."

"Fine."

Her mom shut the door firmly but silently. Julie laid down on the mattress, clothes and makeup still on. She felt exhausted, and hurt, and embarrassed, and guilty, yet somehow invigorated. She imagined once again the angry look on Josh's face, his intensity, and a realization began to take shape: Julie Coleman has something that men want (and want very badly). That thought gave her power.

Before undressing, she opened her phone and typed out a brief message to Josh: "I love you, forever."

Send.

*　*　*　*　*

"Welcome to Starbucks, can I take your order?" Julie smiles, feeling Mary Ann's large warm body brushing up against her.

"Just a small coffee," the woman says.

"Tall drip," Julie says, keying in the order on the register. "That'll be one fifty, please."

The woman hands Julie a credit card and Julie swipes it through the machine.

"Do you need a receipt?"

"No thanks," the woman says, and the coffee appears on the counter next to Julie. Brenda, one of the baristas, excuses herself past Julie and Mary Ann.

"You're already an old pro," Mary Ann says. "Want to try it by yourself?"

"Sure," Julie says. "Piece of cake."

"I'll be in the back, doing inventory," Mary Ann says. "Holler if you need me."

"Will do."

And the customers begin lining up; Julie falls into a routine with Brenda and Lacey, the two baristas. Brenda has brown hair and lots of piercings; Lacey is a blonde, dumpy looking thing. They are both fast workers, Julie notes; sometimes they scold Julie for not ordering loud enough, but other than that, it's like clockwork, or whatever that phrase is, Julie thinks. She begins to savor the sounds and smells of coffee brewing and milk foaming (this is her job now!); she's craving a caramel machiatto and wonders whether it's okay to ask Brenda for one.

Around 10am two men come in, right after one another. The first is wearing a baseball hat and a white t-shirt; the second man is dressed in khaki pants and a polo shirt; he's carrying a laptop shoulder bag.

The man in the baseball hat reaches the counter first; he stares at the drink menu, scanning, his mouth partially open. The second man lines up behind him; Julie notices a tattoo on this man's forearm; at first she thinks it's a number, like from a concentration camp, but then she realizes it's a date. July something.

She wants to ask him what it means, what's so important about one day that you'd tattoo it forever on your body? But the man doesn't return her stare; he simply raises his other arm, places his hand behind the other man's head and--

Crack!

The man's eye explodes.

Toward her.

Julie flinches and gets covered in spray, like from a sneeze.

Crash! A glass coffee pot shatters behind her. The man in the baseball hat slumps over the counter, then slides to the ground; the man with the tattooed arm points a gun downward and shoots again.

Crack!

People scream.

Julie is frozen but feels herself being pulled down, down, down. She lands on her side on the spongy floor mat, amidst broken glass and spilled coffee; the shots are still echoing in her ears. Crack! Crack! Metallic and percussive, painful against her eardrums. Her forearms are spattered with blood and bits of gray and pink. Julie tries to scream but nothing comes out; she huddles against the counter, pushing frantically with her Uggs, and she's surprised to find Brenda there beside her, still gripping Julie's sweater. Brenda has tiny spots of blood on her face too, and a chunk of something white stuck in her hair. Bone? It's all too much, and Julie begins to shut down; she wants to call her mom, or Josh, or 9-1-1, but she's paralyzed, plastered to the ground in a fetal position; she's cold and numb and afraid to close her eyes again, but she can't look at Brenda either, so she stares up at the ceiling, and the brown walls, and the bright halogen lights above her. There is a sharp pain in her ribs, and her ears are ringing; Julie feels herself fading, blacking out; snowflakes shimmer on the edges of her vision; but no, Julie tells herself, no, don't black out! Be stronger than this! She forces herself to concentrate, to focus on something, anything, an object, an anchor, something to keep her from drifting away into darkness, and quickly she finds it, the drawing of the hand turkey from before, the one scribbled in shiny black crayon. She stares at the drawing with every ounce of energy she has left; she burns this image into her soul, recording it over and over again, thinking, "Okay kid, we're in this together now. We can get through this. We can get through anything."

IN BETTER TIMES

Davis goes over the routine one more time in his head: bath, pajamas, brush teeth, read books, lights out. He can do this; it's only two nights. He's watched Kathy put Janna to bed every night for almost three years, and the last six months he's been completely sober.

Janna is sitting on the carpet in the family room, legs splayed beneath her in the shape of a letter "w." She has collected the animals from her Lego play-sets and gathered them inside the Barbie Dream House, which is of course the animal hospital; Barbie herself is the doctor, and all the animals have injuries.

"Help, help, my leg is broke," a lion tells Dr. Barbie.

Davis sits on the ottoman, watching her, trying not to think about the message he saw early this morning. Kathy had been in the shower when her phone began vibrating, scooting across the carpet in their bedroom. And so Davis had picked it up, tapped the screen; maybe it was an update from the airlines or her co-workers. But instead it was only a brief text from her boss: "I can't wait either!" And in his groggy state, Davis had merely set the phone down on the carpet and crawled back into bed. After a few moments, curiosity got the better of him, and he sat up again, determined to read the entire text thread; but right at that same moment, Kathy had finished her shower, was calling to him.

"Honey?"

"Yeah."

"Don't forget to pick up her pink blanket tonight. It's in her cubby at the day care. We need to wash it."

She opened the bathroom door, and the harsh light blinded him, illuminated the room.

"Okay," Davis had said, closing his eyes. "I will."

The opportunity had passed, and half an hour later, Kathy was gone.

Now Davis checks his own phone again; it's 8:04 p.m., and there are no messages from Kathy. No texts. No calls. He scrolls through his contact list and taps a number.

"Hello?" a voice answers.

"I need a drink," Davis tells him.

"That's good," the man says.

"What do you mean, that's good?"

"Say it again."

"I need a drink."

"Perfect."

"Stop messing around," he lowers his voice so that Janna will not hear him. "This is serious."

"I know it is. I've been through it before, remember? But you said 'need,' not 'want.' It's an important distinction."

"The hell it is."

"It means you *want* to stay sober, but physically, or maybe emotionally, you're craving a drink."

80

"Yes. I told you, I need a drink!"

"Okay, well, call me when you WANT a drink."

"You don't understand."

"Goodbye, Davis."

"Dammit. Goodbye."

The Barbie doctor is now the one who's sick; she's on her back in the middle of the Dream House bedroom; the Lego animals are huddled around her, poised to remove her appendix.

"Okay, sweetie," Davis tells Janna. "Time to take a bath."

She turns to him, pleading. "Play Barbies, few more minutes?"

"A few more minutes. And then, it's bath time, little lady."

"Okay."

Davis heads upstairs to fill the tub; he turns on the hot water, full blast, and waits for the stream of water to heat up. To his surprise, Janna appears in the doorway, Barbie in tow.

"No wait! I want to do it," she says. "I want to do it!"

"Do what?"

"Turn the water on."

He shrugs and turns the faucet off.

"Be my guest," he says.

She turns on the cold water, with three quick twists, then runs from the room.

"Where are you going?" he asks; but she's already halfway down the stairs, tiny feet scampering on soft carpet.

Davis tests the water's temperature, then pushes down on the tub's stopper, closing the drain. The water begins to rise.

Why didn't he see this coming? He feels stupid, embarrassed, and yet hopeful that this is just a misunderstanding, a mistake on his part. Maybe the message was sarcastic, or a response to an inside joke: "I sure can't wait for this exciting automotive parts convention." Reply: "I can't wait either!" And then: "LOL."

But inside, he knows.

He knows.

*   *   *   *   *

Forty minutes later, and he's sitting naked in ten inches of bathwater, shivering, holding his knees tightly against his chest; the soap bubbles have long since disappeared; Janna is standing in front of him with her back to him; she is smearing the tiles with pink shampoo.

"Okay Sweetie, time to get out," Davis pleads. "Daddy's freezing."

"Few more minutes," she says, more a statement than a question; she turns to get more shampoo, but slips in the tub; Davis quickly catches her by the arm.

"Whoa," she says. "Close one."

"Please be careful," he says.

He lets go, and for some reason, recalls the first time they touched. Kathy was still in the stirrups; Janna had been weighed but not yet measured; she was swollen and covered in waxy fluids. Davis remembers holding the video camera in his right hand and watching her through the viewfinder. Janna whimpered but did not cry, her arms and legs flailed about, until Davis's left hand entered the frame; he stroked her chest and the side of her arm, trying to soothe her. Then her hand reached toward his; her tiny fingers closed around his index finger, causing the dam inside him to burst. At first, Davis had tried to cry silently, heroically, but soon the camera began shaking and he was openly sobbing, sniffling, and fumbling for the stop button.

"Daddy, I'll make you a picture."

"Okay."

"I need more shampoo."

"We used up all the shampoo."

"I need more." She shakes the empty bottle in his direction.

"Sorry, Honey, that's all we have."

Her voice gets louder, and she starts banging the bottle against the side of the tub. "I need more shampoo! I need more shampoo!"

Davis has had it; he's about to raise his voice at her, when he hears his phone ringing.

"I need more shampoo!"

"Wait! Shhh! Shhhh!" he tells her. "I'll get you more shampoo, just be quiet for a second."

She looks at him expectantly. "More shampoo?"

"Yes, more shampoo. Just, shhh, please!"

The two of them look at each other, waiting; no sound except for the faucet dripping into the tub.

"Dammit," he says.

Davis stands, reaches for a towel. He wants to run, to go get his phone from the bedroom, but knows he can't leave Janna in the tub like this, all by herself.

"I need more shampoo!" she says. "Dammit!"

*   *   *   *   *

9:35 p.m. and Janna is still in the bathtub, fingers and toes perfect white raisins, her long hair wet and dark, pasted to her shoulder blades. He's tried bargaining, promising things, threatening her; but nothing seems to be working. Because now, in addition to body wash, soap, conditioner, and shaving cream, Janna has all her Lego animals and three Barbies submersed in the bathwater--along with a kitchen spatula and two plastic bowls, which are of course boats.

"Here, Daddy, you be the daddy," Janna says, handing him a wet Barbie doll.

"But this is a girl Barbie."

She looks at him, confused. "You be the daddy, Daddy."

"Okay," he says. "I'm the daddy."

"And here, you be the lion too. And the bear. And the bird."

Davis tries to hold all of them at once, but somehow the lion falls, splashes into the tub. For a moment he stares at this toy, this yellow plastic Lego lion, submerged in the tub's tepid water. Something about it seems important, or meaningful, but he can't identify it right now. He can only stare.

"No Daddy, they're not swimming."

"I know, I know," he says, reaching for the lion. "We'll be okay."

*   *   *   *   *

Progress report: Janna is now wearing pajamas (or at least, a nightgown with no underwear), her wet hair is combed, and her fingers and toes are starting to return to normal; all good things; unfortunately, her left arm is now covered with purple scribbles from a magic marker; while Davis was fixing a snack, Janna took the opportunity to draw herself a tattoo--exactly like the one Davis has: Janna's birth-date on his left forearm.

"My fanny hurts." She points between her legs.

"That's not your fanny. Your fanny is back here." He gives her a playful pinch.

"Then what's this?"

"Those are your private parts."

"My private parts?"

"Yes."

"My private parts hurts." She spreads her legs,

and reluctantly Davis looks down.

Her labia are red, inflamed.

"Okay, stay right here." He gets the baby-wipes from the bathroom and returns. "Okay, let's just make sure you're all clean down there."

"Ow," she says. "Ow!"

"Sorry, I'm trying to be gentle." And slowly he dabs at her skin, cleaning out tiny bits of toilet paper. It is a vulnerable moment between them, one in which Davis imagines, if only for an instant, that he is a good father. And a good husband.

*   *   *   *   *

"Okay, I definitely want a drink now," he tells the man on the phone. "Want, want, want!"

"You sure about that?"

"Yes, I'm sure. I'm positive," then, "I think my wife is having an affair."

Silence on the other end, then "I'm sorry."

"Yeah well, I probably deserve it. Look, what if I just had one shot? Just a few swallows of something hard. To calm my nerves."

"Yeah, you could probably do that," the man says. "But here's what will happen: nothing. It won't do a damn thing for you. So you'll have another, surprised that the booze no longer affects you. And before you know it, you'll be halfway through a bottle, and feeling no pain."

"That's all I want right now, to feel no pain."

"So take a nice, hot bath."

"Ha," Davis says. "No thanks."

"Then pray," the man tells him.

"Pray?"

"Pray."

"Is that the best advice you have?"

"It's the *only* advice I have. I can't tell you why it works. I can only tell you it does work."

*   *   *   *   *

10:42 p.m. Davis goes through the routine one more time in his head: bath (check), pajamas (um, check), brush teeth (tomorrow?), read books, then lights out. He's exhausted. Janna is pulling books at random from the bookshelves in her room.

"Ooh, let's read this one!" she squeals. "And this one too."

Soon the floor is covered with children's books: Dr. Seuss, Mickey Mouse, Clifford the Big Red Dog, Winnie the Pooh, Sesame Street, Spongebob Squarepants, Max and Ruby, Curious George, The Berenstain Bears, Dora the Explorer; they just keep coming and coming.

Davis sits cross-legged against the wall, holding his phone with both hands; he's called twice, sent two text messages and one email. So far, nothing in return.

"Daddy let's read this one!" she brings a book to him. Janna plops down in his lap, leans against his chest. "Are you okay, Daddy?"

"Yeah, I'm fine, honey. Fine."

"Are you a sad daddy?" her tone changes to genuine concern; she can sense what he's feeling.

"I'm sorry, Janna. Daddy's just tired," he says, trying to rally for her sake. "But Daddy's always happy to be here with you. You make daddy very, very happy. Let's read a book!" He feigns a smile and it works.

She smiles too. "Read this one!"

"Okay," Davis says, cracking the spine. "Once upon time, there lived..."

*   *   *   *   *

11:23 p.m. She's in Davis's bed now, laying in Kathy's spot; and she's wearing her pink Disney princesses nightgown; it's nappy and softened from multiple washings; the four princesses and their elaborate ball gowns are faded, almost beginning to wear through entirely.

"These princesses," Davis tells her, "have seen better times."

"This one is Ariel," she tells him. "And this one is Cinderella. And this one is Belle. And this one is Jas-mimp."

"Okay, goodnight everyone. Good night princesses. Good night, Janna."

Janna sucks on her sippy-cup, warm milk from the microwave.

"Good night, Daddy."

The lamp on his bedside table is still on, and so are the lights in the upstairs hallway. The rest of the house is dark. His cell phone is nearby, plugged into the wall charger; the message light still unlit.

Janna closes her eyes, and so does Davis. He wants to pray but doesn't know where to begin.

"Daddy?"

"Yes, honey?"

"I need my black shoes."

"No, you don't. Not now. It's bedtime."

"I need my black shoes."

"Janna, you don't need your black shoes."

"Yes I do, I need them."

"We don't wear shoes to bed. Look, Daddy doesn't wear shoes."

"But I need them. I need my black shoes."

"Janna, it's time for bed. No. Absolutely not."

"I need my shoes." She props herself up on all fours and begins to cry.

"Honey, it's late, and you can cry all you want. I'm not getting your black shoes. You need to go to bed. This is ridiculous. I don't care if you cry your eyes out. You need to go to sleep.

It's late. Daddy's very tired, and you need to get some rest. Now go to sleep. Please. Go to sleep."

But this only makes her howl.

"I need my Mommy!" Tears drip from her face onto the bed, and a thin line of saliva spills from her mouth. She rocks back and forth.

"I need my Mommy!"

"No, you don't need your Mommy. Daddy's here. And it's time for bed!"

"I need my Mommy!" tears stream from her eyes and her whole body shudders. "I need my Mommy!"

Davis sits up, sighs.

Where did everything go wrong?

"I need my Mommy!"

He has failed. At marriage. At everything.

"Okay, okay, shhh! I'll get your black shoes, okay? If I get your shoes, will you stop crying?"

She stops sobbing, but the tears continue to flow down her cheeks. She nods.

"And then will you go to bed?"

She nods again.

"Okay, I'll get your shoes. But you have to promise you'll go right to bed. And sleep."

"My black shoes."

"Yes, your black shoes."

She nods, bottom lip curled.

And Davis goes in search of the shiny black shoes, but not before he unplugs the phone from its charger, and dials her number once again.

* * * * *

In the dream he is trying to call Kathy, but the numbers on the phone have been rearranged. They're not even numbers anymore, just symbols or letters. Some of them are missing altogether. And then something soft hits him in the face, like a heavy pillow; he wakes up.

Janna's legs are now over his neck and face. She is sleeping perpendicular to his body. Davis has no idea know what time it is. He turned the clock toward the wall some time ago.

Gently, he lifts Janna's legs and turns her body so that she is parallel to him once again; she stirs but does not wake.

And then, he looks at her, grateful that she is there beside him.

He watches her chest rising and falling as she sleeps; he listens to the sound of her breathing; her nose is slightly congested. She is so close to him, he can feel the heat off her skin, and smell all her smells. Baby shampoo in her hair, fabric softener on her nightgown, and her breath, honeyed by graham crackers and warm milk. But really it's the size of her that amazes him the most; she is small even for her age, to Davis she is not much larger than a bunny rabbit; her spine is as thin and delicate as a string of pearls. Davis counts the features that resemble Kathy's and the ones that resemble his.

They were once in love, and that will never change. Janna is the proof.

He can feel himself falling asleep now.

Fading.

He stares at Janna's face, dreams of her face. Her cheeks glow in this soft light; her skin is iridescent. He reaches out to make sure she is indeed next to him; he strokes her hair gently and tries again to pray.

Not for himself. But for Janna: may she one day grow to have a child of her own.

In response to his touch, she rolls over toward him, spooning her back against his stomach. He kisses her head and rests back on the pillow; a few strands of her hair attach themselves to his beard via cruel static electricity.

He brushes them away, but the hairs return to his jaw, like wispy magnets.

And for a moment, he imagines himself tethered to her; they are connected.

His phone vibrates, but it's muted, distant.

He lets go.

And together they sleep.

JIMMY LAGOWSKI SAVES THE WORLD

Two days before he was scheduled for jury duty
and/or to commit suicide, Jimmy Lagowski received
a postcard in the mail; the handwriting was
feminine, in red looping ink, with no return
address. All it said was, "Jimmy Lagowski, have
you saved the world yet?"

On the front of the card was a starfish
(caption: "Asterina miniata: The Bat Star"); not
the rarest of species, but still, an impressive
display of radial symmetry.

Jimmy stared at the card, its flowery
handwriting. She had found him again, after all
these years.

Dagmar.

But why now? What did she know? Maybe she had
read his mind from thousands of miles away. A long
shot, but he couldn't rule it out. They had
successfully used telepathy (once anyway) when
they were twelve; but that had been eight years
ago, and the two hadn't spoken since.

Jimmy placed the postcard inside the Shoebox of
Destiny (atop the jury summons) and sat in his
underwear on the floor of his bedroom; the room's

white walls began to shimmer, turning silver, so he reached for the oxygen tank, twisted the valve, and held the cannula beneath his nose.

Soon, sweet oxygen was flowing into his body, down the constricted windpipe and into the deeply scarred tissue of his lungs. Instinctively, he brought his hand up to the trachea scar, and ran his fingertips over its tiny, vagina-like shape, thankful that he could now breathe on his own. His fingers continued exploring, finding an edge to the skin grafts and following that edge across his throat and face, all the way to his right ear.

Then, a knock at the door.

"Jimmy?"

"Yeah, mom?"

"You clean those sheets today?"

"No."

(Heavy sigh.) "Land sakes, I give you one simple task."

"Sorry."

"Least you can do is chip in around here."

"Sorry!"

"Don't apologize. Just do it next time."

"Okay. I'm sorry."

"Or I'm gonna' start calling you Slug."

"Okay."

"You want that? Or Sluggo. You hear me? I'm gonna' start calling you that. Sluggo."

"Okay."

She mumbled aloud on her way down the hallway, something about her cross to bear, but Jimmy tuned her out. He switched off the oxygen flow, and flopped onto the bare mattress, which still reeked of urine. There was work to be done. Plans to be made. Only 48 hours left now--not much time, by anyone's standards (Earth or otherwise).

* * * * *

They called each other "douchebag" (or sometimes "douchebucket," depending on who spoke first); and they started their own club within the trailer park; Dagmar was the president, Jimmy was the vice-president and treasurer (two titles, since she'd won the coin toss); for the clubhouse, they'd salvaged an empty refrigerator box and reinforced the seams with silver duct tape; inside she'd hung a Metallica poster and lined the floor with carpet scraps; Jimmy supplied the snacks (bananas!) and toys his mother had brought home from the Salvation Army; together they played with Jimmy's second-hand Star Wars figures, over and over again; Dagmar listened patiently to his stories about the Ceruleans, no matter how many times he told them.

"The world is broken," he told her one day.

Dagmar was laying on her back, blue eyes wide open, each one surrounded by a shotgun blast of brown freckles.

"I said, the world is broken."

"No shit, Sherlock. The world is by definition a broken place."

"Well, I'm going to fix it."

"How? With your Star Wars figures?"

"They're not Star Wars! They're Ceruleans."

"Hmmm. Last I checked, this was Greedo, and Hammerhead, minus a left arm of course."

"No, that's Kevin008 and Larry002. They're on the Council of Elders, and they're deciding the fate of planet Earth."

"Again? What a surprise. Let me guess, they're looking for a Murphy01 Event. But they never find it."

"The Ceruleans are far superior to Earthlings."

"And why is that, Jimmy Lagowski?"

"Because. They're asymmetrical creatures. And that gives them a better idea of what fairness is.

Equality, as they say in Cerulean, is no
substitute for justice."

"You are such a spaz."

"I know you are, but what am I?"

"A douchebag, Jimmy Lagowski. That's what you
are. Just a big, giant douchebag."

"So what? You have freckles."

"Ugh. You're hopeless, Jimmy Lagowski." And
with that she scrambled toward the clubhouse
door/flap.

"Wait," Jimmy had said, or maybe thought, but
it was too late. Dagmar was already sprinting down
the winding road to her trailer, her shoes
crunching on the gravel like breakfast cereal.

*   *   *   *   *

Jimmy awoke slathered in sweat on the bare
mattress. He couldn't recall drifting off to
sleep, but then lately he never did; at some point
in the recent past his dreams had devolved into
mere replicas of his daily life: breathing oxygen,
eating bananas, using the bathroom.

3:45 a.m. Time to go.

The walk to the Coleman Memorial Bridge took
longer than he'd predicted, and Jimmy cursed
himself for not bringing the oxygen caddy; but
then again, he would've called too much attention
to himself, dragging that contraption at this late
hour; better to be slow than obvious.

It was an old bridge, made of concrete, and
pocked by fractures and divots; eroded gaps in the
pavement allowed pedestrians to see straight
through to the iron rebar framework--and in some
cases all the way to the valley below.

Jimmy paused at the memorial plaque; the bronze
inscription told the story of the three men who
lost their lives constructing this bridge nearly

80 years ago; two of them had fallen to their deaths; the other had been crushed by a steel girder. According to the plaque, the structure spanned the Cuyahoga River Valley (nearly half a mile), and connected Summit County with Portage County. At its highest point, the bridge stood almost 200 feet above the valley floor.

Jimmy walked along the bridge's narrow sidewalk, running his hand over the crumbling concrete railing; when he was halfway across, he hoisted himself up and straddled it. The valley beneath the bridge was segmented into three parts: the road (with its adjacent bike path), the river (shallow and gurgling), and the trees (black and foreboding). Jimmy decided to aim for the road; the trees and the water held too many chances for failure, and Jimmy Lagowski had had enough failure in his life.

Using a shard of concrete, he marked the spot where he would jump with an "X."

On his way home, Jimmy paused to catch his breath in front of the local library, the place where Jimmy had taken computer courses with his mom just a few years back; it was also here that Jimmy had mastered the local bus system, its labyrinth of colored routes and timetables. Of course, back then Jimmy had worn the fabric burn mask, restricting blood flow to the scar tissue, and more importantly, hiding his appearance from the world.

Now, as he paused in front of the building's dark windows, he regarded his unmasked appearance. His black hair, once thick and full, was now sparse and riddled with streaks of silver; his brown eyes appeared black and pearled, like a crustacean's. But above all, it was the scar tissue that screamed for attention--pink and thick and relentless.

"Monster."

It had been his 18th birthday, when Jimmy and his mom had taken the bus to the post office, so that Jimmy could register to vote. "It's your duty as an American citizen," his mother had told him. This had been one of the first few times Jimmy had left home without the burn mask; and it would turn out to be the last (at least in the daylight).

Together Jimmy and his mom had filled out the voter registration form, then stood in line. In front of them a young mother struggled to maintain control over her three kids; two of them were swinging on the waiting area's velvet ropes; the other had been clinging to the woman's leg, crying for attention; finally the frazzled mother picked up the child, bringing her face-to-face with Jimmy.

The girl screamed, "Monster!"

The mother turned around. So did nearly everyone else in the post office. Jimmy felt himself blushing, wishing he were back home in the safety of his bedroom.

"Monster!" the girl shrieked again.

"I'm sorry," the woman offered, vaguely in Jimmy's direction. But the little girl was in mid-tantrum; she continued to shriek and cry, which only encouraged the other two kids to join in as well. "Monster!" they all chanted. Embarrassed, the woman excused herself from the line, quickly herding all three children toward the exit.

"Don't you mind them," Jimmy's mom had said. "They're just kids. They don't know any better."

"Everyone is staring," Jimmy had said. "Can we please just go?"

"Oh nonsense," his mother had said, "It's all in your mind." Then to convince him, she said it again.

*   *   *   *   *

"Adults can't be trusted," he told Dagmar. As
usual, she was laying on her back, her fingers
idly picking at a peeling corner on the Metallica
poster. Jimmy could feel the heat of her body next
to his, the comforting weight of her leg resting
atop his thigh.

No response.

"Hey," Jimmy said, "Did you know the Ceruleans
rank adults by wisdom instead of age?"

"Huh."

"Yeah, each Cerulean adult is given a number or
ranking, based on how wise they are. It doesn't
matter how many years they've been alive on the
planet. The numbers are given out by the Elder's
Council. Or maybe they do some kind of
intelligence testing. The point is, they have to
earn their respect. It's not just given to them
because they've reached a certain age."

"Jimmy?"

"Yeah?"

"Can you shut up for a second?"

"Why?"

"Because," Dagmar propped herself up on one
elbow. "I'm sick of hearing about the Ceruleans."

"Okay."

"Don't get me wrong. I like spending time with
you. It's just that, sometimes I wish you'd write
these stories down, instead of telling me the same
ones over and over."

"But my handwriting is terrible."

"And why do the stories always have to end with
Earth being destroyed?"

"I don't know. I guess they don't like how we
treat each other."

"So why can't they just, like, help us or
something? If they're really so superior, why

would they kill us? How is that fixing anything?"

"I don't know. They're just stories, Dagmar. Why are you getting so worked up about it?"

"Because, Jimmy Lagowski. Because."

She sat up, pulling her leg off of his; her head nearly scraped the roof of the clubhouse.

"Let me tell *you* a story for a change. It's about a girl with a messed-up family, and a creepy stepfather who would come into the girl's room at night. Crawl into bed with her. Sometimes, on a good night, he'd only fall asleep next to her, his snoring and beer-breath keeping her up all night. But she had to stay there anyway, because the one time she tried to get up, he choked her."

Jimmy Lagowski sat frozen. This was the most Dagmar had ever said about anything, ever.

"But then the girl started writing it all down in her diary. Only she would change what really happened. So it would end different. Or better. Like maybe the girl would run away from home. Or hide a knife under the pillow. And you know what, Jimmy? One day, it stopped. In real life, I mean. It just stopped."

She pointed to his chest, her eyes brimming with tears. "And that's why you need to write it down."

He wanted to give her a hug, to be strong for her, to let her cry on his shoulder; he wanted to tell her, "I will, Dagmar, I will write it down." But his body was paralyzed by this moment, by its honesty, and by the heat of their two bodies packed together in the cardboard clubhouse, baked from the outside by the summer sun.

"Sorry," was all that came out.

Dagmar shook her head, and turned away from him. "Just forget it, Jimmy Lagowski," she said. "Just forget it."

And this time it was Jimmy who crawled outside

the clubhouse; he stood up, squinted, and without really knowing why, began to run.

* * * * *

It was just after 5:00 a.m. when Jimmy returned home from the bridge; his mother was still sleeping, so Jimmy tiptoed into his bedroom and shut the door. Something about the postcard was bothering him; why didn't she include a return address? Maybe it wasn't from Dagmar after all; maybe his mother had sent it, an attempt to cheer him up?

He inhaled a few good rounds of oxygen then retrieved the Shoebox of Destiny from under the bed; but when he opened the lid, he realized it had been compromised; the jury summons was now folded *on top* of the postcard.

His mom had been through his stuff.

Initial panic turned to annoyance (intrusion!); but Jimmy had anticipated this; that's why all his notes were written in Cerulean code (not that she could read his handwriting anyway). And aside from the postcard and summons, there wasn't much to discover here: three Star Wars figures, an old bus map, two Metallica cassettes, some smashed pennies from the train tracks, and a stack of articles on sea creatures, brain science, and asymmetry, all photocopied at the library.

Jimmy checked the postmark on the reverse side of the starfish card: Los Gatos, California. Definitely not Mom. Maybe it was some kind of game Dagmar was playing: "Find me."

Then Jimmy unfolded the jury duty summons once again, ran his fingers over the gold embossed seal. "Congratulations!" it said. "You have been chosen... not only your civic duty, but an exciting opportunity... arrive by 10:00 a.m. on the date of your summons... lots of people say they enjoyed the process... made lifelong friends..."

From somewhere in the house, pipes came alive, water began running; his mom must be awake now, taking a shower. Jimmy wondered if she would ask him about the summons. He would have to make up something; tell her yes, of course, he would take the #86 downtown to the courthouse; that was the correct bus anyway.

Satisfied, Jimmy packed everything back inside the Shoebox of Destiny and laid down upon the still unmade bed. "Exciting opportunity," Jimmy thought. "That's a good one."

*   *   *   *   *

Jimmy had yanked open the screen door of their trailer home and leapt inside, giddy and out of breath. His mom looked over from the kitchen where she was slicing potatoes.

"Hey Mom, guess what?!"

"What?"

"We started a club! Dagmar and me! She's president and I'm the vice president and the treasurer too! It's awesome!"

"Good for you, Jimmy."

"We're the Douchebags!"

"Pardon me?"

"That's the name of our club, the Douchebags!"

His mom stopped slicing. "Jimmy, do you know what that word means?"

"No, not really. It just sounds cool."

"Well, I suggest you find a dictionary and look it up then." Her expression told the larger story; this was a term Jimmy would no longer be using.

Disappointed, and a little embarrassed, he ran out the door, down the winding gravel road, all the way to Dagmar's trailer. But when she opened the door, her eyes were red, as if she'd been crying.

"I've got some bad news," Jimmy had said.

"Me too," she said.

"You go first."

"No, you."

"Both at the same time?"

"Okay."

"Douchebag is a real thing." / "We're moving."

"What?"

"We're moving. To California."

And so almost immediately they began making plans to run away together--on the Fourth of July, just a few days before the moving truck would arrive. Besides, the trailer park was having a huge party that day; there would be lots of distractions, and all the adults would be drunk.

Over the next few weeks, Jimmy and Dagmar began secreting things away, storing them in the clubhouse. Extra socks. Gum. Spare change. Magazines. A pocketknife. A bar of soap. Everything they would need in their new life together.

July Fourth that year passed slowly; Jimmy spent most of the day inside, watching TV, cursing the clock. Dagmar's family was visiting relatives and didn't arrive home until nighttime.

Around 9:00 p.m. Jimmy finally ventured out. The sky was turning dark and the trailer park's residents were well into the festivities. Red, white and blue streamers fluttered from awnings; radios blared, tuned into the same classic rock station; teenagers snuck between mobile homes, lighting smoke-bombs and firecrackers; partygoers gathered near the park's covered pavilion, smoking cigarettes and drinking cans of Budweiser; Jimmy spotted his mom first, sitting by the bonfire and talking to some neighbors; then he saw Dagmar and her parents by the picnic tables (overflowing with bowls of potato salad, baked beans, and casseroles); Dagmar's mom was slicing watermelon with a long serrated knife; Shane the stepdad was standing beside one of the grills, holding a plastic cup of beer, trying to fan the flames with a paper plate.

Jimmy wandered over toward them and sat on a picnic bench; he tried to get Dagmar's attention, but she was slumped in a chair, pouting. Jimmy figured it had to do with her stepdad, who was pestering her to help out.

"Dagmar," Shane said, "I'm not gonna' ask you again. Bring me that kerosene over there."

"Get it yourself," she replied.

"Dammit, Dagmar. For the last time, bring it over here. Don't make me count to three."

"I'm not your slave!"

"You're about to be grounded, young lady."

Jimmy glared at Dagmar, helplessly. Was she really that stubborn? To risk getting grounded on the very day they were running away together?

"One!" Shane said.

"Dagmar?" Jimmy's voice sounded whiny, even to him.

"Two!"

Dagmar didn't budge.

Jimmy panicked, stood up. "I'll get it for you, Shane."

"Thank you, Jimmy," Shane had said. "You're a good kid. Dagmar, you and I are gonna' have a little talk later." He gestured something to her, which caused Dagmar's mother to raise an eyebrow in suspicion.

Jimmy did as he was told, brought the can of kerosene to Shane, who swallowed the last of his beer before handing Jimmy the empty cup.

"Here, fill this up, Sport."

Jimmy squirted the foul-smelling liquid into the plastic cup. It took several squeezes, but Jimmy managed to fill the entire cup without spilling a drop.

"Now toss it on there," Shane said.

Jimmy looked right into the orange flames and tossed the cup.

Later, they would say that Shane saved Jimmy's life; that if he hadn't thrown Jimmy to the ground and rolled over him, Jimmy may have been burnt beyond salvation; later, they would say that it was a terrible accident, a freak accident, and nobody was at fault; later, they would tell Jimmy he was completely engulfed in flames, over his arm, chest, shoulder, face and head--for what seemed like an eternity; but mercifully, Jimmy did not remember what happened next, his memory stopped recording; it didn't start up again until the EMTs arrived to carry him away on a stretcher; only then would Jimmy recall the torturous pain, the rank smell of his own burnt flesh and hair, and most strangely, the pitch black sky above, where fireworks danced and blossomed in brilliant colors and patterns, in reds and blues and greens and yellows, accompanied by tiny white suns that exploded like popcorn, like cannons.

*   *   *   *   *

Jimmy's mom left for work, without questioning him about the jury summons, and without saying goodbye. Probably best that way, Jimmy thought. He took a shower and put on clean clothes; he also uncapped a new bottle of cologne, Drakkar, a Christmas gift from years ago. Then he sat on the bed, inhaling oxygen and waiting for the three capsules of Albuterol to work their magic on his lungs. Just one quick stop at the library, to type out a proper goodbye, then to the bridge, and the spot marked with an "X."

Outside, the air was warm, the sky blue; Jimmy arrived just as they were unlocking the doors. He marched to the computer terminals, signed in as "J.C. Lagowski," and opened a new document.

But as he began typing, Jimmy couldn't shake the feeling that somebody was watching him, trying to read what he was writing. He kept glancing around, over his shoulder, across the room. Was it a nosy librarian? Another patron? Or maybe a security camera? No, nothing. It was all in his mind. Or maybe it was the Albuterol?

And then a poster on the wall caught his attention, "Denizens of the Deep;" it featured, among other things, various species of brilliant starfish.

Dagmar.

And his unspoken promise to her: "I will."

Jimmy highlighted what he had written so far and pressed the delete button. Then he closed his eyes and waited. It took a while before the words came, but eventually they bubbled to the surface; first in spurts, then in long flowing streams of consciousness. The stories too came back to him, begging to be told; the Ceruleans would find their Murphy01 Event, and Earth would be saved. Jimmy felt the certainty of this moment, as real and tangible as the gold stamp on the jury summons. And soon he was pecking away at the keys with great fervor, creating not just one tomorrow, but two, then several--each one better than the last.

Before printing, he checked the clock on the wall; almost 9:30 a.m.; still plenty of time (at least by Cerulean standards). Back on planet Earth, of course, Jimmy Lagowski had a bus to catch.

WHAT THE PROSECUTOR SAID

"I've placed three items on the rail in front
of you. The first of which is a folded stack of
papers. It looks a little like a hand-written
letter. And in some ways it is. That folded stack
of papers is a eulogy, written by Patrick Coyne on
the occasion of his mother's funeral and burial.
In the eulogy Patrick describes his love for her,
the life lessons he learned from her examples, and
what he will remember about her long after she is
gone. You'll notice that the top portion of the
papers are curled and stained reddish brown. The
stain is dried blood. Patrick's own blood. Because
this stack of papers, this heartfelt eulogy, was
tucked into the breast pocket of Patrick Coyne's
suit-coat, the day of his mother's funeral, the
same occasion where he was shot in the back of the
head, at point-blank range. In full view of his
family and friends, aunts and uncles, nieces and
nephews. The gunshot wound caused Patrick Coyne to
bleed out, on the ground in the cemetery, just a
few feet away from his own mother's gravesite.
 The second item on the rail is a pair of
construction boots, size ten, belonging to Nathan

Coyne, Patrick's brother. You'll notice first of
all the silver duct tape wrapped around the mid-
section of the boots. When the soles had begun to
split, instead of buying new ones, Nate (as his
friends called him) had merely grabbed a roll of
tape and started wrapping. That's the kind of
person Nate was. Proud, practical, humble. Nate
was a handyman, the kind of guy who could fix
anything, and would drop everything he was doing
if you needed his help. On his boots you'll also
notice paint spatters and most abundantly, drops
of Nate's own blood. For Nate too, like his
brother Patrick, was shot in the back of the head
at point blank range, this time in a Starbucks
coffee shop, as Nathan did nothing more than
attempt to order his morning cup of joe.

The third item on the rail links the first two
items together. It is an automatic pistol, a .45-
caliber Springfield DX handgun. The state will
show, beyond a reasonable doubt, that this was in
fact the weapon used in the shootings of both
Patrick Coyne and Nathan Coyne. The state will
also show that this weapon, this .45-caliber
Springfield DX is legally registered to the
defendant, Davis Grant Reilly. Forensic evidence
will demonstrate that the only set of fingerprints
on the handgun belong to the defendant. Ballistic
evidence will connect the bullets recovered from
both crime scenes, the bullets that killed both
men, to the gun you see here. Finally, the state
will provide eye-witness after eye-witness, from
the funeral, from the Starbucks, who will clearly
and unmistakably identify Davis Grant Reilly as
the only possible perpetrator of these shootings.

Before I remove these items from the rail, one
last point of discussion. A very important one. As
you know, the defendant is facing two counts of
first-degree murder, which in Ohio, is defined as

"Killing which is deliberate and premeditated."
And so the burden is upon the state to provide a
motive for these crimes. Why would the defendant
commit these murders, as charged?

The answer is simple: revenge. Make no mistake
about it, the state will show this is a clear and
undeniable case of retribution. Payback for a
tragic accident that occurred many years ago. An
accident which resulted in a jury trial, much like
this one. A trial that ended in a verdict of not-
guilty. In other words, no one was at fault.

But the defendant, not satisfied with the
court's ruling on the matter, chose to take the
law into his own hands. For years, Davis Grant
Reilly planned the murders of these two men,
savoring the idea of retribution, the idea of
their families suffering. The state will present
evidence, taken from the defendant's computer,
from his notebooks, from his credit card receipts
to private investigators, of his plans, his
calculations, and his long-standing desire for
revenge.

Davis Grant Reilly deemed himself judge, jury,
and executioner of these two men. This is
unacceptable. We cannot allow individuals to place
themselves above the ideals of the United States
court system.

And so, when the time comes, I urge you to keep
this case to its facts. These two men, Nathan
("Nate") Coyne and Patrick Coyne, were both shot
in the back of the head at point-blank range with
the same weapon, a 45-caliber Springfield DX,
which belongs to the defendant. Numerous witnesses
will identify a single man, the defendant, as the
only possible perpetrator of these crimes. And
last, the state will provide a clear, undeniable,
and damning motivation for the defendant to commit
these tragic murders.

When the time comes, I urge you to make the right decision. A decision based on the facts. Please, remember Patrick Coyne and the eulogy he wrote for his mother. Please, remember Nathan Coyne and his duct-taped construction boots. These men are gone now, but together we can make sure their deaths are not in vain. I urge you, when the time comes, to do the right thing, and find the defendant, Davis Grant Reilly, guilty of two counts of first-degree murder.

Thank you."

A JURY OF YOUR PEERS

The narrow room began to spin again, and Hank clung to the sides of his chair, scanning the floor for something, a stain or a seam on the carpet, something to focus on, to keep his stomach from heaving.

All around him, people waited for further instruction. An old man with a newspaper folded and re-folded the sports section, doling out an occasional grunt or sigh. A black woman with a flower bonnet thumbed through a paperback novel. And a big, young guy with a badly scarred face, rocked and fidgeted in his seat.

Absently, Hank brought his fingertips up to his own scar, shaped like a number seven, just above his right eyebrow. "Lucky Seven," his friends called him.

The scar: from attempting to spy on Joann Marten at the beach bathhouse when he was twelve years old (epic fail). The nickname: for winning a $1,000 raffle in eighth grade, for sinking a three-pointer in high school to beat arch-rival Holy Name, and for tossing a dart into a bull's-eye in college, from over his shoulder while seated at the bar.

Why was it so hot in here? Hank nearly said aloud.

He was sweating, alcohol sweat, everywhere it seemed. The backs of his pant-legs were soaked; beneath his shirt perspiration trickled down his chest, collecting in his navel; sweat poured from his armpits too, and down his back, soaking into his cotton waistband.

Another woman entered the room and checked in at the desk. This one was older too, sixty-ish, with too much makeup and costume jewelry; she announced her name: Doreen Vincenzo. The clerk thumbed through the computer printout, placing an "x" by Doreen's name, then handed her a blue JUROR badge. Doreen shuffled past Hank, sat down across from him.

The blood was leaving Hank's face now, as if someone pulled a cork in the drain; the backs of his knees were tingling, muscles cramping; his nerves were firing at random and his fingers began to vibrate.

It wouldn't be long now. He was going to be sick, right there in the middle of this musty courthouse waiting room.

"Attention potential jurors," the desk clerk said. "When you hear your name called, please stand up and form a line at the door behind me."

Hank closed his eyes, but that only made things worse. When he opened them, he was vaguely aware of a hand extended in his direction, offering something.

"Tic-tac?" the woman named Doreen was asking. She smiled, revealing a swatch of lipstick on her teeth.

Hank didn't say anything, just held out his hand. Doreen rattled the tiny box and two orange Tic-tacs fell into Hank's palm.

"Thanks," he managed.

He put the Tic-tacs in his mouth, quickly tongued them against his cheek. The saliva came forth, generous and redeeming. He swallowed cautiously, savoring the orange citrus flavor like a drug. And just like that, he had his anchor, his focus. Hank imagined the Tic-tacs as tiny orange suns he had swallowed, or energy pellets from a video game, giving him new life, new health.

When his name was called, Hank stood up, wiped the sweat from his brow, and dutifully stepped into line with the others.

*   *   *   *   *

"All you have to do..." Ted was saying, slumped against the wall, holding his beer, "...is tell them you hate black people."

"Or you think all Mexicans should be shot," Dan added, then gestured with his cue stick, "Far corner." He leaned over, long arms unfolding, and struck the cue ball, much too hard; the nine-ball ricocheted into the pocket, followed immediately by the cue-ball. "Cunt!"

Hank retrieved the white ball from the return slot and paused for a moment, feeling the ball's cold smoothness, its density. He wondered what kind of damage the ball would do, if you smashed it into someone's eye socket. Or struck them in the mouth with it. These were things you had to think about, when you were a man, Hank thought. You never know what can happen in a bar.

The jukebox came to life, pulling Hank's attention away for a moment. A synthesizer, Journey, 1983 "Separate Ways" (*Worlds Apart*). At the jukebox, the girl was still picking out songs. Skinny, with a great ass. A Cleveland Indians t-shirt. Couldn't see her face.

"What if I just tell them," Hank said, "That my two best friends are complete dickheads."

"Hey, just because we went to the same high school doesn't make us friends," said Dan.

"Yeah," replied Ted. "Or dickheads."

"Four-ball in the side," Hank said. He crouched down, reducing the visual field to two dimensions. It was a series of angles now. Math in its purest form. And no one beat Hank at math.

Lucky Seven. He could feel it.

The eleven-ball dropped neatly into the side pocket, and the cue-ball danced off two rails, setting up perfectly for a shot at the eight-ball.

"I'll take another MGD," he told Dan, savoring the taste of victory, one shot early. Dan was the most competitive person he knew, and nothing felt better than beating him at Halo3, or chess, or a game of eight-ball.

Dan frowned, reaching for his wallet.

"And get some shots too, you pussy," Ted said, draining the last of his beer, lazy eye beginning to wander already. "I gotta' take a piss."

Hank took his time lining up the easy shot, and delicately stroked the cue-ball; inertia sent the eight-ball crawling toward the pocket, threatening to run out of steam; the ball hesitated momentarily on the lip, just before dropping down with a satisfactory thud.

"That's game," Hank said. Then he scanned the bar again, looking for the skinny girl with the great ass; he would have to introduce himself.

*   *   *   *   *

They marched through the courthouse, like children on a field trip; Hank focused on the woman's back in front of him, trying not to inhale her perfume. Every sound was amplified in this cold hard space; high heels clicked on the floor; loafers shuffled; men and women cleared their throats, coughed, or sneezed.

The group began ascending a giant marble stairwell, and for a moment hank envisioned them as lambs, being led to the slaughter.

Atop the stairwell, the clerk led them into an open courtroom, where an audience was already gathered, along with a defendant, attorneys, bailiff, two stenographers, and a judge. Behind the judge on the wall was an enormous seal of the State of Ohio, and flanked on either side of him were flags of the United States.

"Welcome, everyone," the judge said, smiling. "And good morning."

The clerk herded the first twelve people into the juror's box, announcing each seat number as the person sat down. When the box was full, she opened a reserved partition of the audience section and instructed the others to sit in the order they had lined up.

Hank was #17, and thankful he was not seated in the jury box. That thing was like a stage, and the courtroom's audience was focused on them, almost accusing them. The black woman with the bonnet. The old man with the newspaper. The guy with the scarred face. Doreen Vincenzo. This was the real thing; the real deal. Hank thought maybe they were headed to another waiting room. Not a trial in progress.

He was thankful too, for the Tic-tacs and the stroll through the marbled courthouse. His leg muscles were no longer cramping, and the sweat on his body was now being pleasantly cooled by the room's generous air-conditioning. And maybe it was his imagination, but the four ibuprofen he swallowed before leaving the apartment were finally kicking in, at long last reducing the swelling inside his brain.

To Hank, the defendant looked like a regular person, aside from the orange jumpsuit of course. In different clothes, this guy would blend into the background of friends or relatives or total strangers. Invisible, hank thought. Just like me.

While the judge began reading instructions, Hank tried to piece together the previous night. Epic night, Ted would say. Holy shit, what were they thinking? It made Hank grin.

When Hank looked up at the judge again, it appeared the man was staring directly at him, frowning a bit. Hank nodded, pretended to listen. The judge was still reading instructions; he mentioned the phrase "a jury of your peers," and Hank's foggy mind wandered once again.

Paul Simon, "Still Crazy After All These Years," 1975. The lyrics from the title track:

> *"...But I would not be convicted*
> *by a jury of my peers,*
> *still crazy after all these years."*

That song began to play in his head while the prosecutor stood up to begin her jury selection questions. She was smartly dressed, in a yellow dress suit, with thin features and pale freckled skin; her reddish brown hair was pulled back tightly into a bun, and she wore small glasses with almond shaped frames.

Hank wondered what this woman would look like naked: would her nipples be small and pink? He thought so. Would she shave her pubic hair into a thin strip or a nice, neat triangle? He wondered too, what would she taste like? What sounds would she make in bed? He imagined himself, fucking her doggie-style, pulling her red hair tight, then turning her around, so he could come on her face,

114

right on her fancy designer glasses.

But instead of arousing him, these thoughts make his stomach turn. This time, it wasn't the alcohol. More like some kind of guilt. Or regret. What had happened last night?

Fragments came back to him: introducing himself to the chick in the Indians t-shirt (what was her name? no idea); doing lemon drops with that chick and her friends; doing Irish car bombs; shots of Jaegermeister (Ted); then drinking vodka Red-bulls to stay awake; and smoking cigarettes (uh-oh) outside the bar with the girl, telling her that he was a "party smoker"; inviting the girl and her friend to play pool with them; arguing with Ted over not calling his shots; wanting to fight Ted, thinking about punching him, the guy was so damn competitive; Dan's lazy eye getting lazier; and then, and then!, betting the girl that he could make an impossible double-bank shot: "If I can make this shot," he told her, "you have to make out with me." He hiccupped and she laughed; then he spent a good three minutes lining up the shot, marking the green felt with dashes of blue chalk. Hank could see the shot in his mind, the angles, the spin; Lucky Seven!; he couldn't miss; but when he stroked the cue-ball, it jumped into the air and bounced off the table; must've forgotten to chalk the cue-stick. Ted could not stop laughing, and Hank snapped the pool cue in two pieces over his knee.

Guns n' Roses, "You Could Be Mine", 1991.

The pool stick. Was that why they got kicked out? There was an angry bouncer escorting them to the door, pulling Hank by the collar. Was it for breaking the cue stick? No, they played another game after that, or several games in fact; then Ted busted a bottle against the wall, right in front of the bouncer--that was it; that's why they were kicked out!

But then, one more thing: Hank had puked too at some point. He threw up in the bar's bathroom. When did that happen? Sometime after smoking the cigarette. He didn't even make it to the toilet, threw up the moment he entered the bathroom, then finished in the sink. And why was he still holding a cue-ball? He dropped the white ball into the garbage can and splashed water over his face, tried to clean himself up; then Ted came in, tackling him into the wall. Or no, before that, the girl had been in there with him, in the men's room. Hank definitely remembered the girl's angry face, the bathroom stall doors behind her; she was yelling at him for something; what was she so mad about? Was it the bet he made? Or the broken pool stick? He had no idea. And for that matter, what was the girl doing in the men's bathroom!?

What a night. Epic night indeed.

> "...But I would not be convicted
> by a jury of my peers,
> still crazy after all these years."

The female prosecutor asked her next question: "Has anyone here ever been convicted of a felony or misdemeanor?"

A thin, homely woman in the juror's box raised her hand, nervously giggling.

"I was."

"Can you tell us about it?"

"Sure," she laughed again. "It was a failure to appear in court. I got a ticket for a noise violation, for playing my music too loud, and I forgot to send in the fine until it was too late."

"Did you get an attorney for this?"

"Nope."

"Okay, well, thank you. Anyone else, convicted

of a misdemeanor or felony?"

A man in Hank's row raised his hand, waved to her.

"Yes?"

"I have a D.U.I."

"Can you tell us, what were the circumstances?"

"Well, I had had a couple pops that night, and I was driving home from the bar, and I came to a stoplight. Then I realized I had no business being behind the wheel, so I crawled into the back seat and fell asleep. A police officer woke me up by knocking on the window."

"He wasn't too happy I'll bet."

"No ma'am."

"So what did you say to him?"

"I asked him what happened to my driver."

The courtroom erupted in laughter. Hank included. His shirt and pants were beginning to dry now, sweat evaporating in the cooler climate of this room.

"Your honor?" the defense attorney stood up. He was a short man, with brown curly hair and mismatched clothing: green pants, yellow shirt, and blue blazer. "I'd like to request a short break."

"Can I ask your reason?" the judge replied.

"I'm sorry, your honor. I need to use the restroom. Too many Diet Cokes this morning."

"Fifteen minute recess," the judge said. "I want everyone back in their seats by 11:30 a.m." He tapped the gavel twice, and everyone stood.

Hank stretched and wandered out into the hallway, turned on his cell phone. No messages. He opened a text thread to Dan and typed: "Epic night."

Send.

Almost instantly his phone vibrated, incoming call from Dan.

"Dude," Hank answered.

"Dude! What the hell happened last night?"

"You tell me!"

"Holy shit, you were wasted."

"I know. Total blackout."

"What did you say to that chick?"

"What chick, the Indians t-shirt?"

"Yeah! The one who thought you were raping her."

"What? What are you talking about?!"

"She told the bouncer you threatened her with a cue-ball."

"Are you serious!?"

"Yes, I'm serious, dipwad. You followed her into the women's bathroom, and told her to make out with you or you were gonna smash her face in with the cue-ball."

"Holy shit. I don't remember any of that. I didn't say that."

"Dude, that's messed up. The bouncer had you, like by the collar, he was gonna call the cops and shit, until Ted busted that bottle against the wall. Then we all ran like crazy."

"Wow."

"Yeah."

"Jesus."

"Look dude, I gotta run. I'm late for a meeting. Call me later."

"Alright. Hey, sorry."

"No worries, man."

"Alright, later."

"Later."

Hank closed the phone, frozen in disbelief. All around him, people with juror badges mingled or made phone calls. The defense attorney emerged from the bathroom, tucking his yellow shirt into this green pants; there was a piece of toilet paper stuck to the man's shoe; it fluttered behind him as he returned to the courtroom.

There's no way. No fucking way. That chick must've been a psycho. There's no way he threatened her like that. Maybe she was drunker than they were. But still... Fuck! Shit! Not on his drunkest night. There's no fucking way. No fucking way in hell.

*   *   *   *   *

One by one, the lawyers excused jurors from their duties. Just about everyone who spoke up was asked to leave. The woman who played her music too loud, the man who got a DUI, even a guy in a suit who merely asked how long this whole trial would take. In total, eleven people were dismissed from the room.

Hank discreetly opened his cell phone and texted to Ted this time: "Call me!" Then he slipped the phone back into his pocket.

"Juror Number Seventeen," the clerk said, "Please move up into the juror's box." At first, Hank did not make the connection, but everyone it seemed was looking at him, expectantly.

"Pardon me?" he said.

"Please be seated in the juror's box, at seat number twelve," the judge echoed. Hank nodded and stood. Inside his pocket, the phone was vibrating, and Hank shuffled along the floor, trying to obscure the noise.

He sat down in the juror's box, waved to the others, to Doreen, the old man, the woman with the bonnet, the kid with the scarred face. Hank was now seated directly across from the defendant, who was slumped in his chair, eyes toward the floor. The orange jumpsuit was stained, and hung loosely on the man's frame.

Guy looks guilty as hell, Hank thought.

Whatever he did.

The judge thanked the remaining potential jurors, excused them from the courtroom, then offered more instructions to those seated in the juror's box. They were to meet in this courtroom at 9:30 a.m. the following day. They were not to discuss any elements of the trial with anyone, even with each other. They were to remain impartial, and remember that every defendant is innocent until proven guilty...

When they were dismissed, Hank stepped outside the courthouse and stretched; he un-tucked his shirt and turned his cell phone off; he didn't feel like talking anymore. About last night or anything else. He wanted to disappear. He wanted a drink.

Across the street were two bars; Hank chose the smaller one, the one on the right. Inside were a few regulars who squinted against the light, plus a jukebox, a few tables, and dozens of framed Irish quotes and jokes.

Hank bellied up to the bar. The place would do. It was no different from any other bar in the world. Just a place where people come in, become invisible for a short time, then leave. We're all just pawns in someone else's game, Hank thought. Everyone marching forward, without ever knowing or understanding why.

The bartender, a bald man with unruly eyebrows, slapped a napkin down on the bar, nodded.

"Miller Genuine Draft," Hank said. He glanced at the television briefly, war in the Mid-East, another celebrity in trouble, tornado damage.

"Do you mind if I play the jukebox?" Hank asked the bartender.

"Naw, go ahead. Plug it in first."

Hank found the cord and plugged the machine into the wall. Instantly it lit up, pink and blue and white, motors and gears whirring. A7, B12, F9, C13, they were all possibilities, The Doors, The Who, Pink Floyd, Led Zeppelin, but he kept searching. That song was stuck in his head now, and the only way to get rid of it was to play it in its entirety. Maybe twice. So he scanned the titles, sure that he would discover it. If only he searched for a long enough time. If only he tried a little harder this time, things would fall into place once again. "Come on," Hank said to himself, "Come on, Lucky Seven."

DOREEN VINCENZO, LESBIAN

She didn't like the sound of it, not one bit,
any more than she liked the prosecutor's smug
attitude, the way this woman was always talking
down to them, like if the jury didn't agree with
her, they must be so stupid.

Doreen preferred the erratic defense attorney,
with his unruly hair and his wrinkled, mismatched
clothing. She imagined the man getting dressed in
the morning, fumbling through a dark bedroom,
being ever so careful not to wake his kind yet
homely wife.

Lesbian.

The word was unflattering to her, and yet
somehow thrilling. Like a giggle in church or a
middle finger kept beneath the dashboard. And
maybe that's what had attracted Doreen to Roxie in
the first place. Maybe at age sixty Doreen needed
more thrills in her life; too much time spent
worrying, keeping her lip buttoned, always
wondering what everybody else was thinking.

Regardless, Doreen had made the right choice by
ending things. The proper decision, Father Joseph
would say, upon reflection. Doreen would find her

thrills another way.

When the lunch break was over, the defense attorney resumed his questioning; he released the psychiatrist and called an expert in neuroscience. This doctor's list of credentials was long and very impressive. Many published articles. Many grants and awards. Doreen sat forward, turned her notebook to a fresh page, and cocked her pencil.

More exhibits, entered into evidence. This time they were MRI brain scans; black scans illuminated by vibrant splotches of red, blue, yellow, orange, and green. The first set of scans was a control set, taken while patients merely relaxed in the scanning device. The second set of scans, the doctor explained, were functional MRI scans, taken while patients conducted various tasks to determine which parts of the brain were most active during the execution of those tasks.

Doreen scribbled furiously. She imagined herself on an episode of "CSI," reporting this information to Gil Grissom.

The doctor calmly elaborated on the study (Vanderbilt: Buckholtz, 2008), its acceptance and credentials (*Neuron, Scientific American*), as well as its predecessor (Princeton: Greene et al 2004), which in turn was supported by a grant from the National Institute of Health. "We now know with almost complete certainty which areas of the brain are most active during moral and legal decisions," the doctor said. "Judgements of right versus wrong."

"Can you tell us what those areas are?" the defense attorney asked.

"Of course. The strongest correlations occur in two areas: the right dorsolateral prefrontal cortex (rDLPFC), which seems to govern questions of fairness and responsibility, as well as the amygdala, which seems to be strongly associated with questions of consequence or punishment."

Doreen lifted her pencil from the page. When she looked up, the defense attorney was looking straight at her. Kind eyes. Tired eyes. He hadn't slept in days.

"And Doctor," the attorney said, "Would you mind spelling those terms for us?"

Doreen blushed, smiling a little bit. A few jurors in the box giggled. This jury duty thing was just what Doreen needed, a distraction. Something to keep her mind busy. Away from you-know-what. And you-know-who.

*   *   *   *   *

The sky was black now, its stars so numerous even the largest constellations were hard to discern: the Big Dipper, Orion the Hunter, Cassiopeia. The air was calm; the smells of Ohio farm country, the animals and their manure, had already sunken back to earth. There was only the smoke from the fire-pit, and an occasional, distant whiff of skunk.

Doreen and Roxie sat together on a two-person swing, sharing a blanket over their lap; in front of them, a circle of bed-and-breakfast guests took turns drawing cards out of a copper bucket; it was a game the B-n-B owner had made up years ago, she said. "An ice-breaker. To get folks talking."

When it was Doreen's turn, she tried to politely pass, but the circle egged her on.

Reluctantly, she rose and drew a card from the bucket, read it silently to herself.

"What is the best day of your life?"

The card was initially stuck to another, and Doreen pried them apart with a fingernail. The other card said "most embarrassing" something or other and Doreen dropped it into the bucket. Phew, that was a close one.

She read her card aloud, then turned to face the circle of guests, eagerly awaiting her response.

"Probably today," she said, surprised by the swiftness and volume of her answer.

Then she resumed her place next to Roxie on the swing, too quickly perhaps. The boards creaked and the swing jerked unevenly, its chains clicking. Roxie spread the blanket over their laps again, then reached for Doreen's hand and squeezed.

It was true.

"I'll pick you up at 10:00 a.m.," Roxie had said. "And bring a toothbrush." Doreen had spent most of the morning trying to decide what to wear. Something casual, but nice. This wasn't exactly a date, just two friends taking a day-trip. But still. She didn't want Roxie to think she was a slob (or a snob!).

So white chinos and a printed top it was, but when Doreen answered the door, she knew she had chosen poorly. Roxie was standing there, dressed in jeans and a black leather vest. Behind her, on the street, was Roxie's Harley Davidson motorcycle, resting on its kickstand.

"I guess I'll be wearing jeans then," Doreen said, and they both laughed.

Doreen had never been on a motorcycle before. At first, she could only hold onto Roxie, laughing nervously and crouching tightly against Roxie's warm back. The interstate was positively frightening; trucks never seemed so monstrous, cars too, and the wind would not stop screaming through the tiny openings in her helmet.

Doreen didn't open her eyes until she felt the bike slowing; they veered off onto an exit ramp and headed toward country roads, state routes; now instead of four lanes there were two; instead of going 70 mph they were doing 50 mph; and instead of semi-trucks there were farm tractors and hay-bailers.

Amish country.

Doreen had driven through this part of Ohio before, but that had been in a car. Inside a safe, enclosed, climate-controlled environment. This was quite different. They were part of the country, one with it, and yet moving through it somehow. There were no artificial dividers between Doreen and the perfect blue sky, the green sloped hills, the red barns and silver silos, the swaying cornfields, the horses and the cows.

It was exciting. It was invigorating. It was like being on a rollercoaster, but without the harness, without the pre-determined track.

The road curved left then right, up then down, always changing, always moving. From time to time, they would approach and overcome an Amish buggy. Roxie would swing the bike out wide to the left and Doreen would wave as they passed. She saw Amish men with their telltale beards and black hats. Amish women wearing bonnets and hand-sewn dresses. Kids waved back at her, smiling, even cheering at the speeding motorcycle.

Doreen squeezed Roxie tightly and hoped the ride would never end.

Around noon, they stopped at a country-style restaurant for shoo-fly pie (Roxie's idea). Then they visited a local flea market (Doreen's idea). While they separated for a moment to browse the tables, Doreen took advantage to buy Roxie a small gift, a hand-crafted black leather bracelet; she stashed it inside her purse; Doreen would give it to Roxie later, as a memento of their trip.

But when the two reunited, Roxie offered a different opinion of the place: "A bunch of junk, sold to you by people with fleas."

"Oh goodness," Doreen said; she smiled politely, clenched her purse shut.

*   *   *   *   *

"The Catholic Church," Father Thomas said, "has been very clear on this matter." He paused to take another bite of his Big Mac, and wipe his mouth with a napkin. The man was dressed casually today, and Doreen struggled to keep imagining him as an authority figure; she wanted black robes and a white sash; she got jeans and a pink golf shirt. "And even, proactive, when you think about it," Father Thomas said. "In 1986, the church issued a formal statement on the matter, addressing gay people, their struggles, and their persecution."

Doreen blushed. She felt like everyone in the Mcdonald's was listening in on their conversation. Father Thomas was always a loud talker; perhaps from his constant presence on the altar. She sipped her Diet Coke, pinching the straw, bending it, while he continued.

"It's not a sin to be gay. And the church welcomes gay people with open arms. But you have to understand, God created man and woman in his image, as two complimentary parts meant to unite under the sacrament of marriage and further the Lord's creation. So *any* sex outside that union is sinful, including gay sex."

A nearby table of teenage boys laughed out loud. One of the boys spewed Coke out of his nose. Doreen tried to convince herself they were laughing about something else, but it was useless.

She began clearing her tray. The sooner she got out of here the better.

Father Thomas suppressed a burp and continued. "So if someone commits an act of gay sex, they must confess their sins under the Sacrament of

Reconciliation. They must be absolved by a priest."

Doreen stood, wiped a wet spot on the table with a napkin. "And if they don't, confess?"

Father Thomas began gathering his own tray. "Well, like any sin, God will judge and decide. It depends on how often the sin occurred, and whether they were truly sorry for their transgressions. So depending on the person's other merits, we're probably talking Purgatory versus Hell. But still, not Heaven."

"I see."

Behind the counter, the deep-fry alarm sounded, as if to emphasize his point.

In the parking lot of the Mcdonald's, Doreen called Roxie and broke up with her. She explained the church's viewpoint, and that although she very much enjoyed Roxie's company, she didn't wish to see her again.

The other end of the line was silent for a moment, and Doreen wondered what Roxie was doing, and whether she was crying.

"Sorry about that, Darling. I went to get my calculator."

"Pardon me?"

"I couldn't find my calculator. I have a few questions for you, Reenie."

"Okay?"

"At what age do you think a person is free to choose their own religion? Meaning, they are mature enough and knowledgeable enough to choose a spiritual path for life?"

"I don't know. Eighteen?"

"Aw, skidmarks! I didn't know I liked women until I was twenty-six! But okay. Let's use eighteen. Next question: How often did your parents bring you to church as a kid?"

"I don't know, once a week. But not always."

"So, three times a month?"

"Something like that."

"Plus Christmas and Easter?"

"Yup."

"What about other services? Like weddings? Funerals? Baptisms? Ash Tuesdays? All those things. About how many of those did you go to a year?"

"Okay, I get it. We went to church a lot."

"Hold on a second."

Doreen waited patiently while Roxie punched in numbers on the calculator.

"Okay, here's my point. By the time you were 18 years old, you spent over 1,000 hours in church. That's more than 40 straight days. And that doesn't even include all the class time you spent in Catholic schools, learning about Jesus, Mary, and Joseph. Or the fact that your two biggest holidays include a shit-ton of toys and candy for little kids. So with all that, do you really feel at age 18 you were free and unbiased to choose your own spiritual path?"

"If you're trying to tell me I was brainwashed, I'm hanging up."

"Not brain-washed, Darling. Faith-washed."

"Good-bye, Roxie. I'm very sorry."

*　*　*　*　*

That bracelet was still in her purse, and Doreen wondered now, sitting in the juror's box, whether she should just throw the dang thing away. She wondered too, what impulse had propelled her to buy the bracelet in the first place; it was unlike anything she'd ever purchased before: a black leather band with two silver skulls on it; when you fastened the snap, the skulls faced each other, like they were staring each other down. Or,

Doreen thought, like they were about to kiss.

It was stupid.

Doreen turned her focus to the defendant in his orange jumpsuit; the man looked so relaxed, he almost appeared to be sleeping. Doreen wondered what the man would look like in different clothes. Like Father Thomas, would he be a completely different person?

With the judge's permission, the defense attorney entered another slide into evidence, then began addressing the expert witness again.

"Can you please tell us what this slide is, labeled F-023?"

"That's a three-dimensional model of the brain."

"And if you could, please tell us about these highlighted regions?"

"Yes, the region in blue is the hippocampus. The region in yellow is the prefrontal cortex, and the region in red is the amygdala."

"And what is the significance of those highlighted areas?"

"Those are the parts of the brain whose functions are most affected by post-traumatic stress disorder. During a PTSD episode, the hypothalamus secretes an excess of hormones, which causes hyper-arousal of the amygdala, and insufficient top-down control by the pre-frontal cortex and hippocampus."

Doreen wrote "PTSD" in all caps. Then drew a box around it. The attorney continued.

"And what does that mean... in plain English, Doctor?"

"It means the amygdala, or excuse me, it means the emotions hi-jack the brain, and kick reason out of the pilot's seat."

"So during a PTSD episode like that, is it safe to say, a person would not know the difference between right and wrong?"

"Objection your honor!" the prosecutor slammed her pen down on the desk.

"Sustained," the judge said. Then to the defense attorney, "Counselor, you should know better. Please re-phrase."

"Apologies, your honor," the attorney said, clasping his hands together. Then, to the witness: "Doctor, is it possible that during a PTSD episode, those same regions of the brain which we discussed earlier, the regions that are most active during evaluations of right and wrong, are significantly impaired?"

"Yes, I think it's more than possible. I think it's extremely likely."

"Thank you. No further questions."

Doreen drew a question mark after the words "right and wrong." And then another.

And a third.

*   *   *   *   *

That night Doreen dreamed about brain scans. And about Purgatory. She dreamed she was on some kind of operating table in the hospital, surrounded by doctors and nurse, including Father Thomas, dressed as a surgeon, but wearing a thick wooden rosary atop his scrubs.

"Doreen," Father Thomas said. "It's time to get started." He placed his hands upon her head. "Please, say your Act of Contrition."

Doreen began reciting, the words from Saint Mary's grade school still deeply etched into her memory, "My god, I am sorry for my sins with all my heart..."

When she spoke, bright colors emanated from the overhead lights, dancing around the operating room. Blue, red, and yellow. It was beautiful. And the colors were somehow coming from her!

She continued reciting, "In choosing to do wrong, and failing to do good, I have sinned against You, whom I should love above all things. I firmly intend, with Your help, to do penance, to sin no more, and to avoid whatever leads me to sin. Amen."

The room was awash in bright primary colors, like a muted concert stage. The doctors nodded to each other; this was surely a good sign.

But when Doreen looked at Father Thomas, he was frowning. She had failed him somehow.

"Doreen, there's something you need to confess."

"I haven't done anything wrong."

"You've stolen something from us," the priest said. The other doctors nodded solemnly.

"I didn't steal anything," Doreen said. But one of the machines in the room began to sound an alarm, an urgent beeping, a lie detector? "I've never stolen anything."

"We need it back, Doreen," Father/Doctor Thomas said. The beeping sound got louder and louder until Doreen woke up.

She must have set the alarm clock by accident. Today was Saturday.

Doreen sat up on the edge of the bed, stretched, and took a sip of water; then she retrieved her purse from the dresser. Digging through it, she found the black leather bracelet. The band with the two skulls. The clasp had come undone, and Doreen snapped it together again, forming a perfect circle.

Then she dialed the phone.

Sometime around noon, she heard Roxie's motorcycle pull into the driveway. This time Doreen was ready, with black boots and jeans. Roxie waved as Doreen came down the steps.

"You sure?" she asked Doreen.

Doreen nodded, and reached for Roxie's bare wrist; Doreen fastened the bracelet, noting how perfectly it fit; just enough room for wiggle; the two silver skulls were now facing each other once again. Like they were kissing.

"Oh cool!" Roxie said. "I love it!" she handed Doreen the passenger helmet, and helped pull the chin-strap tight.

Doreen placed a boot on the foot-peg and swung her other leg over the seat; she could feel the heat coming off the bike's exhaust pipe, even through her jeans. So she adjusted her feet on the pegs and reached forward, holding onto Roxie's waist. Doreen would love this woman. She would never let go.

"Ready," she said.

"Um, where are we going?" Roxie asked.

"It doesn't matter," Doreen said, above the bike's rumbling motor. "Just go."

Roxie shrugged and eased the bike into gear, guiding them out of the driveway and onto the street. Doreen smiled, imagining her brain inside its skull lighting up like a rainbow. Like the most perfect sunset. Like the heaven she might never know.

THE ACCIDENT IN QUESTION

In the year 2000, the U.S. National Park System officially designated the Cuyahoga Valley as a protected area (Ohio's first national park!) to be preserved for the enjoyment of its visitors. Covering more than 33,000 acres of land between Akron and Cleveland (mainly the valleys surrounding the northern flowing portion of the Cuyahoga River), the park features many popular visitor attractions, such as the scenic Ohio/Erie Canal (and its towpath), a historic valley railway system, Brandywine Falls, covered bridges, rock ledges, beaver marshes and various lakes--plus 125 miles of hiking, biking, and horseback trails.

From the air, this valley system resembles a jagged, gaping wound, as if the earth's soft underbelly were torn open by the talons of a giant, mythical raptor; and its tempting to think of it that way, even for a geologist such as myself. Sometimes there is comfort to a myth, or a story like that, one that cannot be duplicated with facts or science.

I was the park superintendent that day, when the accident happened, the one in question.

In the N.P.S. management-training program, they tell you to be prepared for anything, which is entirely correct.

And of course, impossible.

For the previous ten years, I had been stationed at Mammoth Cave, Kentucky, spending most of my days underground, studying limestone formations and measuring natural gases, when I received the offer. Three factors contributed to my decision; first, I was tired of living in the dark, dank womb of the earth; second, I have family here (my parents are deceased, but I am fairly close to an aunt and two cousins; we share a meal at Thanksgiving and exchange pleasantries around the holidays); third, and perhaps most telling, I was deeply fascinated by the unique story of this region, its contours, its rocks.

The Cuyahoga Valley National Park is a quintessential example of a buried glacial valley; and it called to me, like the ocean calls to a sailor, or one might even say, like a lover calls to another.

From a geological standpoint then, this story begins in ancient Pangaea, during the Paleozoic era, some 250 million years ago. At the time, this area of northeast Ohio was entirely submerged under a great lake, bounded on all sides by the super-continent, and located just south of the equator. As a result, most of the surface rocks in the park are sedimentary, stratified layers upon layers of sand, silt, marine minerals, and clay that hardened over time to become sandstone, limestone, and petroleum-rich shale.

But of course, this was merely the beginning. During the Jurassic period, Pangaea began to break apart, and the North American tectonic plate drifted. Gradually, inch by inch, year by year, this continent crept northward toward its current location, covering a distance of 2,000+ miles. It is maddening to comprehend the scales involved here; the earth and its processes can be infinitely patient (and mind-bogglingly slow).

At some point along the journey, the North American plate collided with two underlying plates to the east, causing a different kind of movement: upward. The continent began ascending; the vast and deep lake that covered Ohio receded to lower lying areas, leaving behind a complex network of tributaries, comparable to the modern-day Mississippi delta.

As we've seen in other national park systems, such as the Grand Canyon and the Badlands of South Dakota, when a river moves atop sedimentary rock, the water begins to carve its way downward, revealing tall bands of sedimentary beds. The results can be quite astonishing and quite dramatic! The biggest difference in Ohio is the composition of the rocks themselves; a greater proportion of shale and quartz has produced cliffs of dark gray with an occasional twinkle of mineral.

And then, about two million years ago, a remarkable event occurred; it wasn't the first time, and wouldn't be the last. The earth experienced a major global cooling period, which would come to be known as an ice age. Mathematician and engineer Milutin Milankovic has perhaps explained this phenomena best, "...as a rare (and cyclical) combination of orbital eccentricity (location of the sun within earth's elliptical path), axial tilt (degree to which the earth's axis leans toward the sun), and axial precession (a gyroscope-like meandering caused by rotational velocity)." Long story short: a smaller portion of the earth was exposed to sunlight, and for a shorter period of time.

Massive continental ice-sheets accumulated in Canada and drifted southward into the states, masking roughly two-thirds of Ohio. Like a steamroller, these mile-thick ice sheets flattened everything in their paths, ironing out any dramatic features; and like a bulldozer, the sheets dozed massive amounts of soil, rocks, and boulders into Ohio's valley system, filling the ravines with over 1,600 feet of displaced material. Dozens of metamorphic rocks (gneiss, marble, mica, etc), never before seen in this area, found a new home in the Cuyahoga Valley.

When the cooling period abated, these immense sheets of ice shrank and retreated into Canada, leaving behind ponds and lakes, as well as swiftly moving streams of melted glacial run-off; combined with the newly displaced soil and rocks (glacial moraine), these streams sought out new paths, joining forces to create the strange and v-shaped river known as the Cuyahoga.

Finally, as the earth warmed, and the climate's familiar cycles returned, the Cuyahoga Valley sprang to life. The displaced soil would prove quite fertile, fostering deciduous trees (oak, elm, maple, hickory, beech), evergreens (pines and spruces), and various species of plants, shrubs, and wildflowers. Birds and small animals found shelter and sustenance here, feeding off insects, berries and nuts; but their existence was not without adversity. The harsh winter conditions at this longitude forced the development of survival strategies. And so the animals that remain here today have adapted to survive the region's deadly freeze/thaw cycles; insects such as the honeybee cluster together at the bottom of the hive surrounding the queen, consuming honey for energy, and rotating their positions for warmth; cold-blooded amphibians, reptiles, and fish merely slow down, establishing an equilibrium with the cooler temperatures, and burrowing if necessary to keep from freezing to death; passerines (perching birds) migrate south to warmer climates; although some birds like the robin and the cardinal remain throughout the winter, simply switching from a diet of worms and insects to a fare of seeds and nuts; smaller mammals like bats and woodchucks hibernate; others, like deer and squirrels, merely reduce their activity as well as their intake. Animals it seem, show a knack for adaptation to their environment--a genius some might say, rivaled only by the crafty Homo sapiens.

It is possible (or even probable) to suggest that human beings roamed this region for the past ten thousand years; but their nomadic, hunter-gatherer lifestyle left little impact upon the land (as well as few fossils and artifacts); it wasn't until the Adena tribe of Native Americans settled in the Cuyahoga Valley nearly three thousand years ago that we begin to see the tell-tale signs of human activity and civilization.

The Adena were farmers and extensive traders; they relied on the Cuyahoga for transport from Lake Erie to the Tuscarawas and Mahoning rivers and eventually the mighty Ohio (of course, this was long before the Ohio/Erie Canal was dug by hand as a shortcut). The Adena were also artisans; they painted, capturing various aspects of their lives and culture on pottery and stone tablets; fragments from these objects remain today, many of which are on display in the visitor's center of this park. But above all, the Adena are best known for the curious burial mounds they left behind; for the Adena (like most native Americans) were polytheists, worshipping many gods, and practicing a form of shamanism for communication with the spiritual world; the Adena believed in reincarnation and the transformation of humans into animals (and back again). And perhaps it was this belief in the afterlife which drove them to honor the dead with massive burial mounds (some 20 feet tall and 300 feet in diameter); the mounds remain, scattered throughout Ohio today; the Adena and their zoomorphic gods have been for the most part forgotten.

August 13, 2002, started like every other day that summer. In the morning, I recorded the day's temperature, humidity, dew point, and barometric pressure; nothing unusual stands out for me; by noon the temperature had already peaked at 92 degrees F and the humidity at 74 percent, which is quite common for this region at that time of year. It was a muggy day, and almost certainly I reminded my colleagues to keep an eye out for dehydrated hikers and/or victims of heat stroke.

Sometime around 2:00 p.m., I was taking samples from the pond at White Tail Marsh, when my radio erupted, spoiling the moment's silence, and causing at least one blue heron nearby to take flight.

The call was from 9-1-1 dispatch: "Proceed immediately to Settler's Cove, for a possible 570."

If you are a park superintendent, 570 not a term you ever want to hear. It's the park system's equivalent for "Code Blue" or "Code 99" in a hospital. I dropped the sample tubes and ran to my truck.

Settler's Cove is primarily a family destination with expansive grassy stretches, picnic tables and barbecue grills; that particular portion of the river is calm and shallow (not a drowning); there are no steep ledges from which to fall; I kept telling myself it must be a heart attack; someone at the pavilion perhaps. Truth be

140

told, I hoped it would be a heart attack; I found
myself wishing for this, and mentally prepping
myself for CPR and first-aid, as I drove the truck
as fast as was safe, its yellow siren flashing but
mute.

By the time I got there, it was over.

In the grass near the shore, a small crowd of
people had gathered, huddled around a man who was
sitting on the ground, holding something in his
lap. This I could see even through the windshield
of the truck as I skidded to a stop. I grabbed the
emergency pack, kicked open my door, and began
running toward the scene; for some reason this
particular moment comes back to me in dreams; it
haunts me, this uncertainty, not yet knowing what
had happened, but ultimately being responsible for
whatever it might be; I was panicking; I was
running; even now I can clearly recall thinking
how the air, impossibly thick with humidity, was
slowing my every step; like I was running in slow
motion; or perhaps time itself had slowed down, as
it does when approaching an event horizon.

There was no need to run, after all. The child
was dead.

She lay in her father's lap, a bloody mess. The
man sobbed and sobbed; it is a sound I will never
forget, inhuman and deeply primal.

I dropped the emergency pack and called the
dispatcher on my radio; I confirmed the report and
requested a 620 (the euphemistic term for
coroner), and cancelled the ambulance, which
showed up a few moments later anyway, along with
two police cruisers.

At this point, I hadn't even noticed the three
brothers and the dog, who had huddled together
under the nearby pavilion. Only after the police
officers took control of the scene and began
asking questions did I register their presence.

The entire incident probably took less than a minute or two. And maybe that's why the witness accounts were so markedly different; only later, after we compared notes and stories, could we identify the similarities and the differences. What follows is the best we could gather.

The man and his three-year-old daughter were flying a kite, the kind you buy at a store like Wal-Mart or Target. The kite was shaped like a ladybug; although the two were not having much luck, the girl nevertheless squealed with delight on each subsequent pass.

Nearby, the three brothers I mentioned were drinking beer (which is illegal in the park), and taking turns throwing a stick into the river for their dog to retrieve (another red flag: dogs must be on leashes at all times). Technically, this dog, a Staffordshire bull terrier, was on a leash; but none of the men were holding onto the other end.

At a certain point, one of the brothers slipped while tossing the stick, his sneaker's sole losing purchase on the smooth, wet shale; the man fell backwards onto a rotted log, partially smashing a hive of honeybees; as before, this particular species of insect has acquired some pretty unique survival strategies; for instance, when the hive is threatened, the bees secrete a pheromone, a signal to all the hive members to exit their home, and attack the threat.

And so a swarm of bees attacked the fallen brother first, followed by the dog second. At first the dog only yelped and nipped helplessly at the air; but then the animal began to run; unsure of what was happening to it, and where the pain was coming from, the dog could only focus its attention on the squealing girl, as she ran and ran, laughing, unraveling kite string; her father stood a good distance away, also laughing, still oblivious to what was happening nearby.

The dog took her down; it seized her by the neck, clamped down, and shook violently; quite possibly her neck was broken instantly. At this point we can only surmise, and only hope. Regardless, she began to scream and choke; her father ran toward them, which only made the dog bolt in the opposite direction; two brothers also gave chase, but the animal was too fast, even with the additional weight of the child. They chased and chased, while the girl screamed and screamed. The men collided with each other, diving for the dog's leash, to no avail; the dog escaped their efforts, dashing across the bike path, into the forest and back again; finally, the dog must have tired; it paused, facing its pursuers, and gave one last powerful shake, which nearly separated the child's head from her body, and the screaming stopped.

The brothers tackled the dog and pinned it to the ground, all of them panting. The man sat on the ground, trying to hold his daughter together, telling her it was going to be okay; it was all over now. But the life was gone from her, and her face was covered in blood and dog slobber and dirt, her expression frozen in fear; the man closed her eyes, and just sat there on the ground, gently stroking her hair. Only when the crowd began gathering around him did he begin to wail.

In hindsight, the ambulance was useful after all; the two EMTs needed to sedate the man before he would give up his daughter; we all assisted, each one of us assigned to a limb; I had the left arm, and I tried to focus on the man's tattoo while he bucked and swore at us; the tattoo was a date, and blood was smeared over the black ink; only when his body began to go limp could I look into his eyes; red and swollen and wet; his eyes rolled back into his head, then returned; in a moment of clarity, he locked eyes with me, and uttered a single word, "Why?"; then after an instant, his eyes rolled back again, and he was out.

I didn't have an answer for him; I could only shake my head. Years later, I still don't have an answer; perhaps there is no answer to a question like that; and perhaps that is why I am still haunted by dreams, always running toward the crowd by the river, and never sure what I will find when I get there; always I am slowed, I am paralyzed, I am petrified.

The next day, an anonymous person erected a small, white cross near the banks of the river at Settler's Cove. Soon the flowers came; the notes and photographs; the toys and stuffed animals. This growing shrine became a daily stop for me, another agenda item for the park's manager; it seemed like there were always flowers to be replaced, notes and photographs to be collected and re-hung; before long I found myself sealing the photos in Ziploc bags, making Xerox copies of the notes, so that when one page faded or smeared, another could appear in its place; surprisingly, the stuffed animals were the biggest problem; over the winter they became water-logged and frozen and dirty; in the spring they hatched mold and fungus and began to smell; insects and animals moved in (as they will) and began devouring them; in the summer birds sat on the crossbeam of the shrine and shit all over everything; but still, everyday I cleaned; this went on for quite some time, in fact all the way to 2010, when I resigned from the position; I took down the shrine, packed everything up into a box and buried it in the nearby silt and clay; it only seemed right; I still visit that spot at Settler's Cove, the spot where I buried the shrine; I even say her name out loud.

Janna.

Of course, she doesn't answer; but there is nevertheless a comfort in talking to her, and I have found a habit or routine in this one-way conversation; so I ask her questions about her day. Or about her family. That sort of thing. Sometimes I'll talk about myself, the fading memories of my parents, or the loneliness to which certain paths may lead; if I'm feeling especially chatty, I will tell her what I know, the long and patient history of rocks; and I will whisper questions to her, like when is the next ice age coming? Or what will become of this area and its valleys? Will the continents collide again? What happens to our planet in a million years? Of course, as before, she does not reply.

What could she possibly say?

THE CURIOUS DISAPPEARANCE
OF JAMES C. LAGOWSKI

The bus was late. How many times had he waited at this exact same stop in the past month? Fifteen? Twenty? More? Each weekday, same time, same stop. And now, this! What would happen to him if he were late? Would they kick him off the jury? Or swap in an alternate? Jimmy Lagowski hoped not. He was determined to see this thing through its end; the trial and his search for Dagmar were all that kept him going these days.

This was not good.

Jimmy adjusted the dial on his new portable oxygen concentrator, decreasing the pulse-dose from three to one; the new LED indicators showed two green lights, less than two hours of battery power remaining; he didn't have time to fully charge the unit this morning, running late to catch this bus, which was itself late, by a whopping twelve minutes.

Not good, not good, not good.

Come on bus, Jimmy thought once again; as if he could beckon public transportation with telepathy; anything beat just sitting here on this wooden bench in this crappy bus shelter, helpless against the sadistic whims of the bus gods. The pavement beneath his enormous feet was riddled with black gum spots and cigarette butts; to his right a poster advertised an insurance company, featuring a caveman with a club; if Jimmy held his head in just the right position, he could superimpose his own scarred reflection on the caveman's body; it seemed fitting.

He grunted.

In his left rear pocket was the essay he wrote and printed at the library over the weekend, "The Scales of Justice;" it was Jimmy's best attempt to answer the foreman's barrage of questions: how could one person possibly be worth more than another? What criteria could we even use to measure that sort of thing? And anyway, who are we to determine what's right and wrong?

"Our job," the man said, "is to follow the judge's instructions to the best of our abilities."

"But what if we disagree with those instructions?" Jimmy asked. "Or their definitions?"

"That's not up for debate," the man had said.

Jimmy tried to elaborate on the spot, but all that came out were fragments and ramblings, metaphors, half-baked loaves of bread; Jimmy stuttered; he panicked; he sneezed uncontrollably. Other jurors looked on with pity or disbelief; a few rolled their eyes, as if Jimmy weren't sitting right there. The foreman strongly encouraged Jimmy to reconsider his point of view, and trust the judgement of the other eleven people on the jury, all of whom were in strong agreement: "Guilty." The foreman suggested they resume at 9:00 a.m. Monday morning, when surely, clearer heads would prevail.

And now this. Was this some kind of fate? Or predetermined destiny? If so, whose fate was it? Jimmy's? Or the man who was on trial?

For the umpteenth time, he retrieved the bus schedule (right back pocket) and scanned the highlighted column; the 8:23 still hadn't arrived; the next bus wasn't due until 8:53, fifteen minutes from now; that bus would reach downtown at 9:20; and then, he would still have to catch the loop to reach the courthouse; or he could hoof it for eight blocks, but even the thought made him tired; not to mention, there was the issue of the battery power in his oxygen concentrator; he cursed himself for not bringing the charger.

This was shaping up to be a real shit-fest.

What would Dagmar do? Good question. Maybe the only question. Jimmy's inability to locate her weighed more heavily on him with each passing day; everything was connected; his life was an infinitely scattered puzzle which could be solved only by finding the key piece: Dagmar.

She would improvise. That's what Dagmar would do. She would refuse to accept someone else's destiny. There are thousands of paths to the same destination; if one is not working, we simply choose another; otherwise we stop moving; otherwise we die.

And so Jimmy Lagowski stood up, left the comfort and safety of the bus shelter. He shuffled to the curb and, facing oncoming traffic, held out his thumb.

A few cars slowed or honked, possibly frightened by the sight of this large, scarred young man holding a weird mechanical device, but soon a small black sedan pulled to the curb; the driver waved Jimmy forward.

The man's name was Paul, or maybe Pat, and he drove Jimmy all the way downtown, to within five blocks of the courthouse; Jimmy told him about the essay, about his situation; the man apologized for not taking Jimmy all the way, but he was running late as well. He wished Jimmy good luck and honked as he drove away.

So close now. Jimmy was sure he could make it. He increased the flow of oxygen to the maximum dosage, and steeling himself, slowly, awkwardly, began to run across the concrete sidewalks of downtown Akron. Almost immediately his knees began to ache, his thighs slowing him with each scissor motion; his feet were literally being pounded into the ground; hard soled shoes, so painful!

The portable oxygen concentrator slapped against his hipbone, and he struggled to hold it there while he ran. The blood rushed into his cheeks, heating them instantly; the blood thundered inside his head; then a traffic signal.

Stop! A steady line of cars and trucks passed by in front of him.

He paused, waiting for the light to turn green again; his chest burned; his lungs wheezed; it seemed like forever before the signal changed, and the "Walk" sign finally illuminated; Jimmy resumed his journey, past the parking garages and office buildings, briefly colliding with another man on the sidewalk, apologizing; he could see the courthouse now, just three blocks away; the sculpture in front, the blindfolded woman holding the scales, was two-inches tall; Jimmy focused on that sculpture; everything else melted away.

But inside, Jimmy was fading, the power shutting down; sweat ran down his temples, down his back; silver flakes appeared on the edges of his vision; he had to rest; something was wrong; he slowed to a walk, then stopped moving entirely.

The oxygen machine was running at full strength, still one green LED indicator glowing;

but the plastic tube leading to the cannula had come undone; he must have knocked it out while running. Jimmy knelt down to fix it, placing one knee on the sidewalk; panting heavily now; his hands seemed so far away from him, the tube's opening impossibly small; and before he knew it, Jimmy was laying flat on his side, warm sidewalk under his skin; his head struck the pavement just above his left ear; one final gaze toward the justice statue, now six inches tall, now sideways, and Jimmy was out.

*   *   *   *   *

"We're closing," Jeanine told the young man at the library's computer terminals. "In ten minutes." The blunt tone in her voice surprised her. Any other day and she would've had more patience, more compassion; half of this guy's face and neck were badly scarred, probably from a fire; any other day, yes, but not today; not after eight years of marriage; fuck him, fuck everybody; we all have our crosses to bear, Jeanine thought; scars run just as deep on the inside, maybe deeper.

"I'm almost done," the young man said. He typed slowly, finger-pecking, with great determination and focus. When he finished the current sentence, he looked up, eyes hopeful, pleading.

"Did you have any luck?" he asked her.

"Nope. No Dagmar Jones in Pacific Grove, California. No Dagmar Jones anywhere in California. Or in the United States for that matter. Sorry."

Jeanine tossed the starfish postcard on the table next to him.

"Here, you can have this back."

"Is there anything else we can try?" he asked.

"Nope, sorry." In truth, there were a hundred other things they could try; but Jeanine had her own problems to deal with; she didn't want to spend one more minute working on someone else's problems. That was her biggest flaw, thinking she could help people, thinking she could fix things. Not anymore. "Maybe this woman got married. Changed her name."

The young man snickered. "I don't think she's the marrying type."

Jeanine could barely hide her annoyance. "And what exactly, in your opinion, is the marrying type?"

"I don't know. The kind who don't argue much."

"Sounds like you don't have the slightest clue about marriage," Jeanine could've stopped there but didn't, "Or anything for that matter."

"I'm sorry," the young man said. "I didn't mean to offend you."

"Look, just finish up," she had said, trying on her new role as the ice queen. "Print what you have and shut down. It's time to go."

* * * * *

Jimmy awoke in a hospital bed, pulling at the tubes in his arm; his skin was sweat-pasted to a thin blue cotton gown; beside the bed, an IV-bag with clear fluids rocked gently from its metal hanger; an oxygen flow machine compressed and beeped; a blood-oxygen monitor clamped down on his right index finger; and several EKG patches were stuck to his chest; all familiar sights and sounds; familiar room even; small and narrow, with dark green curtains; this was City Hospital; Jimmy reached for the call button and pressed it.

A few moments later a nurse appeared, carrying a glass of water.

"What time is it?" Jimmy asked her.

"About one-thirty," she said, offering him the water. "How are you doing?"

"Okay," he said, sipping from the cup. "What happened?"

"You had a hypoxic episode, fell down. The doctors wanted to run some tests, take some pictures, make sure you're okay."

"What tests?"

She picked up his chart, flipped a page.

"CD4 Count, Hemoglobin A1C, and some x-rays of your noggin. As soon as you're feeling up to it, of course."

Jimmy set the cup on the tray and reached for the lump above his ear; no pain, in fact, no pain anywhere; must be morphine in the drip; also familiar.

"I need to go somewhere."

"Negative, my friend. Not until the doctors give the okay."

"Then I need to call somebody."

"The courthouse? I think they already called for you."

"They did?"

"Well no, the EMTs called for you. They found the number in your back pocket. Along with your other stuff."

"Here," she said, reaching to the bedside table, handing Jimmy his wallet, jury summons, bus schedule, and a brand new yellow post-it note.

"Where's the essay?"

"I don't know. This is everything they found in your pockets."

"We have to find it!"

"If it helps at all, they took a message for you."

Jimmy read the note: "From courthouse: sorry to hear news. Alternate juror will be selected. Don't worry about trial. Focus on your health." Jimmy read the note a second time, the lines vibrating ever so slightly. What would happen now? Was it all over? Jimmy looked up at the nurse and without warning began to cry.

*   *   *   *   *

"Poor Jeanine," her mom had said over the phone. "Poor, poor Jeanine." And then, out of nowhere, a spear thrown, "Maybe if you'd been a little more affectionate..."

"Affectionate?" Jeanine had barked. "What the hell is that supposed to mean?"

"Don't get upset now. I'm not pointing any fingers. You know the women in this family have a hard time communicating their feelings."

"Gee, I wonder why. I'm hanging up now, Mom."

"Yes, run away Jeanine. Run away from your problems."

"I'm late for work. Goodbye, Mom."

Two hours later, she found herself trying to stay busy, re-shelving books, sending emails, making phone calls, trying to fill her mind with anything other than the following: cheating, separation agreement, trying to make things work, everything happens for a reason, I don't know if I love you anymore, let's discuss this like adults, and maybe worst of all, there are things about her that remind me of you, when we first met.

Ugh.

And so when she came across the young man's name on the computer log-in sheet, she assigned herself a task: she would help him find this Dagmar Jones. She would distract herself with this quest; she hadn't recognized his name before; the staff knew him better as "The Brainiac," the guy who checked out every book in the library on the human brain, and then had more transferred from surrounding libraries; Jeanine imagined the conversation when she saw him again; first she would apologize for being such an unruly bitch. Then she would announce: I've got good news for you. I found her.

The man's scarred face would light up; perhaps tears would fall. "Oh thank you, thank you so much. You have no idea what this means to me."

Jeanine would amass a string of good deeds, like individual pearls on a necklace. And maybe that would be enough. Maybe.

But Dagmar Jones proved to be more elusive than first thought. Even Jeanine's friend in the State Records department could find no match. No marriage certificate. No death certificate. Just a birth certificate confirming what Jeanine already knew; the woman was alive somewhere on the planet.

From her desk, she stared at the rubber tree plant in the lobby; an old man walked by with a cane; she followed him, wondering what it will be like to grow old alone; stop that, Jeanine; it's not over yet; she was 35 years young; Christ, just saying it like that made her feel old.

And then her gaze came to rest on one of the library's many posters, "Denizens of the Deep," and in particular one of the red, chubby starfish toward the bottom, "Bat Star." The same type of starfish that appeared on the front of the young man's postcard.

She Googled it. Found a wikipedia page. "Latin name: Asterina miniata... wide variety of solid and mottled colors... has webbing between arms like a bat... normally five appendages but can have as many as nine... abundant in central California and Monterey Bay... fights with other bat stars, in battles that last several hours, each bat star trying to get an arm on top of its foes... can only be seen through sped-up video footage..."

Jeanine returned to Google: "Bat Star Monterey Bay." The first link was an advertisement for the Monterey Bay Aquarium, a new exhibit devoted to entirely to bat stars. "The world's largest collection," the ad said.

Jeanine paused for a moment, then picked up the phone.

*   *   *   *   *

Jimmy went through the plan in his head: call the courthouse, stop them from using an alternate juror, then get to the courthouse somehow, show them the essay--but first, he needed to find the essay. Where was the essay? And holy balls, this morphine was strong.

So hard to focus.

Maybe he could call the library, print out another copy; but no, he had deleted the file, trashed it; the librarian had been angry with him.

He had to find the original. Where could it be?

He sat up, and the room came with him, tilted on its fulcrum. Jimmy was tethered to this bed, this room, by at least four devices: the oxygen machine, the finger monitor, the EKG patches (four of them), and the IV-drip; he could easily disconnect the oxygen tube and IV-line; but the EKG and pulse monitor had alarms attached to them; if he disconnected them, the nurse's station would be alerted; and even if he did figure out a way to detach, there was still the issue of leaving the hospital; he had to make his way past the nurse's station to the elevators, then down through registration and lobby, past the security guards, out the front door; and Jimmy Lagowski wasn't exactly the type to blend in; his huge body and scarred face practically screamed the opposite.

Think, Jimmy. Think.

He surveyed the room, searching for something, anything to help him. The television and its remote (batteries), the green curtains (and a drawstring), table beside him, with phone, lamp and extension cord, his puffer, his pulse-dose oxygen concentrator, lunch tray on a collapsible stand (sandwich, pasta salad, Jello cup, cookie), a wheelchair (folded); on the wall facing him, the television in its bracket, a painting of sunflowers, the light switch, and a mercury thermostat.

Jimmy closed his eyes and leaned back in the bed again. Shapes floated through the darkness, wires dangled, begging to be connected; images from the past called to him; used and broken toys his mother had brought home from the Salvation Army: an erector set; a potato clock; walkie-talkies; he scanned through the images until he found what he was looking for--a dusty, square box with a mutilated cover: "12 Fun and Exciting Wiring Experiments!"

In his mind, Jimmy opened the box, reached inside.

*   *   *   *   *

When the meeting was over, Paul Thompkins walked outside the office for a break. He needed a walk. Or a cigarette. Maybe both. What a bunch of bullcrap. Two weeks of work down the drain. All because some jackass client changed his mind.

Paul loosened his tie and crossed the street, toward the parking lot. He waved to the attendant and unlocked his car. The front seat was scorching hot, and Paul reached into the passenger's side, opening the glove compartment for his cigarettes and a lighter.

On the floor was a white envelope with a huge brown footprint on it. Paul picked it up, opened it. Probably from the guy this morning, the one he had given a ride to. The guy with the badly scarred face.

The pages inside were stapled together. Some kind of essay or dissertation. The cover page was titled, "The Scales of Justice." Paul folded the paper, put it back in the envelope, and tucked the envelope into his breast pocket. He'd throw it away at work, forget all about it.

But then, no. Then he wouldn't be any different than the jackass client; that poor fellow probably worked hard on this thing; he deserved better.

Paul slapped the cigarette pack against his palm, twice, three times, packing the tobacco; then he pinched a cigarette and lit the end, savoring that first blast of warm, spicy air. Almost instantly his blood tingled with nicotine. It was time for a little walk.

*   *   *   *   *

The nurse paused in the doorway of Room 403A, unsure of what to think. The room was warm, extremely warm; the thermostat cover was missing; but most peculiarly by far was the lack of a patient, one James C. Lagowski. All the machines were still there, the EKG, the pulse monitor, the oxygen compressor; even the IV-bag and stand stood there proudly, watching over the bed; but there was no patient! Instead, in his place, the strangest contraption the nurse had ever seen: what looked like the motherboard of a computer, with a tangled mess of wires attached to it; and the weirdest part of all: at the center of this thing, this bizarre contraption, was a cup of red

Jello, which pulsed rhythmically, not unlike a
human heart.

*   *   *   *   *

After three rings, a man answered. "Good
morning, Monterey Bay Aquarium. Can I help you?"
   "Can I speak to Dagmar Jones please?"
   "Sorry, we don't allow personal calls."
   "Can you confirm that she works there?"
   "No, I'm sorry. I cannot."
   "Okay," Jeanine said, momentarily stumped.
   "Anything else I can help you with?"
   "No, but thank you."
   "Alright then. Thanks for calling."
   "Wait, can you transfer me, to the new starfish
exhibit, the one with the bat stars?"
   "One moment please."
   The line went silent for a moment, followed by
a soft click.
   "Hello?" a voice said, "This is Dagmar."

THE SCALES OF JUSTICE
(AN ESSAY)

Small questions have small answers. So if you had asked me, what band rocks your socks off? The answer is easy: Metallica! Or another, what is the greatest movie ever made? *Star Wars* (Episode Four, the original; George Lucas started in the right place, then 20 years later punched everyone in the nuts).

Even objective questions follow this rule: what is the only fruit that exhibits trilateral symmetry? A: Bananas! (An obscure reference to be sure, but as you can see, there is only one correct answer, and it is a short one.)

On the flip side, BIG questions have big answers. Lengthy answers. Complicated answers. And sometimes the only way to get at them is to cut the question up into little pieces, like it's a giant chocolate cake or something--oh man, cake sounds so good right now--and then cut those pieces up again and again and again, until we have bite-sized cake pieces that everyone will agree are oh so delicious and satisfying.

The big questions are like that: when does human life begin? How big is the universe? What the jizz is art? How does nuclear fusion work? What happens after we die?

So maybe now you can understand why I had such a hard time answering your question on the spot, for your question is as big as questions get. (As an aside, I apologize once again for sneezing on you, repeatedly; this is a nervous tic I acquired at some point in my life for who knows what reason; the doctors call it "stress-induced rhinitis," a histamine-reaction brought on by the hormone cortisol; but nevertheless it continues to plague me and embarrass me in social situations! So, once again, I am sorry. If there are any dry-cleaning bills let me know and I will gladly pay for them. As long as they are not too expensive.)

Okay, phew! Now onto your question: "How could some people be worth more than others?"

In hindsight, I realize that my reply "They just are" was not sufficient; nor were my ramblings on the egregious errors of our nation's Declaration of Independence appropriate for that setting. These are matters for another time. Or another essay. Because, well, shit.

The answer to your question is not self-evident, because your question is one of value, and therefore must include some kind of scale, context, and measurement. This sentence right now is a test to see if you're still reading; if you gave up because you were bored, then go stick your head in a bag full of dicks; as for the rest of you, my fellow jury members, the ones still reading, please accept my apologies for crudeness; trust me, after a group of doctors tell you that you have less than six months to live, your patience and tolerance are among the first ones to pack their bags and get the fuck out of Dodge.

The value of anything found in nature (raw materials, commodities, or resources, as opposed to manufactured goods or currency exchanges) derives from its scarcity/rarity (like rhodium), its utility/usefulness (fresh water), or some combination of the above (oil, duh).

So the first cut to the cake is this: what makes human beings rare?

To simplify things, let's stick with what we know: earth and its inhabitants; physically, there are animals on this planet which supersede humans in almost every way; cheetahs are faster, elephants are bigger, bears are stronger, hawks can see better, frogs can hold their breath longer, even cockroaches may be better equipped to handle extreme environmental conditions.

Only when we switch the discussion to the mental world ("smarts"), do human beings begin to emerge in this context as truly unique, rare, and exceptional.

Most scientists will tell you that there are at least three methods for determining intelligence in any animal: 1. Sheer size and complexity (folding) of the brain itself, 2. Relative brain size to total body mass, and 3. Amount of brain development from birth to full maturity (capacity for learning).

By all accounts humans kick major ass, and with a size-13 combat boot (steel-toed, my good friend). Our brains are at least three times larger than any other animal with a comparable size/body mass (even our closest relative, the chimpanzee, with whom we share 98.5 percent DNA, has a brain about the size of an orange; compare that to our cantaloupe); the only exceptions here include the bottlenose dolphin, which has a slightly larger brain, but also a significantly larger body mass (450-650 pounds); elephants too possess an enormous (and complex) brain, but once you factor in their freaking huge-ity, elephants fall off the scale entirely.

As an aside, I have always thought that dolphins are adorable. Don't you think they are cute? Of course you do! How could you not?! They are the slippery, rubbery darlings of the animal kingdom. It's hard to imagine striking a dolphin with a baseball bat or a set of nun-chucks (something that cannot be said about sharks and most camels); but I digress...

The human brain is made up of 100 billion nerve cells (as many stars in the Milky Way, or as many galaxies in the universe; so in summary, I guess, a shit-ton of nerve cells); this makes the number of potential brain states staggeringly vast, almost incomprehensible, except of course by a species like Homo sapiens. If I am blowing your mind right now, just wait; it gets better. (Music up: guitar solo).

As everyone knows, it wasn't always like this; millions of years of adaptation have shaped and grown the Homo sapient brain into a magnificent, complex, and dynamic organ, which is biologically unique in the animal kingdom.

For starters, most of our brain's growth and expansion has taken place in the cerebral cortex (sometimes called the new brain, as opposed to the structures we share with lizards and squirrels, the old brain). So large and rapid was the expansion, the brain organ was forced to begin folding within its confined space, resulting in the cauliflower-like appearance we all know and love. The cerebral cortex is the seat of higher thought in humans, where our most complex mental functions are carried out.

So if you've ever wondered what makes humans

human (and even what makes you YOU), guess what home-slice? Today is your lucky em-effing day.

1. An expanded set of frontal lobes (within the cerebral cortex). These areas of the brain issue simple motor commands, plan actions (kinda cool), and help you sort and maintain a hierarchy of goals and values (super cool); the frontal lobes also handle your working memory or short-term memory, logical reasoning, and conceptual aspects of the self (like, I'm a fat dying virgin, fuck you very much).

2. Within the frontal lobes, humans also boast an unusually large prefrontal cortex; this area is totes important; the prefrontal cortex governs ambition, empathy, foresight, personality expression, a sense of morality, social behavior, and a sense of dignity. No wonder some scientists call this area of the brain "the seat of humanity." In fact, if your friend Joel damaged his prefrontal cortex, no doubt by riding his moped into a stop sign (fucking Joel), you might say afterward, "Joel no longer seems like Joel." And you'd be right.

3. Wernicke's area. This portion of the bean is located in the left temporal lobe (also within the cerebral cortex; see the pattern here?). In human beings this region has ballooned to nearly seven times the size of the same area within a chimp's brain; so it won't surprise you when I tell you that Wernicke's area controls the comprehension of meaning and the semantic aspects of language. The man was right: we think, therefore we are. Ka-pow!

4. A complex occipital lobe. Not entirely unique by itself, but combine that with 30 different areas for visual processing (instead of a mere dozen in most mammals), and you get a visually dominant species. Our brains are hard-wired to detect movement, gauge perspective,

process color, recognize faces, evaluate safety/danger, estimate depth/height, and so much more; hundreds if not thousands of feedback loops help us determine what we are looking at, where it is in relation to us, and most uniquely "So what does that mean to me?" N.B. If you are thinking about designing your own android and/or sweet robot, I recommend studying this area; don't cut corners; you'll gimm it up for sure.

5. The inferior parietal lobules (the IPLs); this region grew so much that over time it split to form two entirely new regions, another anomaly among the animal kingdom; in a broad sense the IPLs help you create a mental model and spatial layout of your surroundings (along with your place in them); these lobes are crucial for math, abstract thinking, and language; as if that weren't enough, the IPLs also control action planning and sequencing; they allow you to conjure up vivid images of intended actions then orchestrate them. Point of fact: Einstein's brain had huge IPLs; what does that tell you, bitches?

All these things taken separately, are incredible; collectively, they are even more impressive. In the broadest sense then, here is what makes the human experience rare and unique on planet earth:

A. Greater range of conscious experience

No wait, let me change that. The GREATEST range of conscious experience. No other animal plans, sorts, expresses, behaves, comprehends, remembers, creates, reasons, empathizes, believes, predicts, composes, evaluates, imagines, calculates, emotes, intends, prioritizes, wonders, or understands quite like we do. This unparalleled range of conscious experience is what makes human life so remarkable; it's also why we value dolphins and chimpanzees more than cattle and rainbow trout;

and why nobody feels bad about swatting a fly. Stupid flies!

B. Vast and complex communication system

Other animals live in communities or social networks; they communicate verbally and non-verbally. But human beings alone possess vocabularies of thousands of words (as opposed to dozens), express themselves in flexible, rule-based syntax (sentence structures); and only humans express and extract meaning. Together these qualities enable us to share complex thoughts, ideas, and strategies with future generations. Or at least, that is the hope.

C. The ability to detach

At some point in our evolution, the human brain acquired an infinitely fascinating and globally unique skill: the ability to detach from one's objective, present point-of-view (the self) and visit other worlds, other minds, even other times. The rest of the animal kingdom is tethered to the present POV, constantly evaluating their environment, acting on instinct and implicit memory, focused on survival and the task at hand; only human beings can uncouple (detach, explore, and return); we relive experiential memories, we wonder what others are thinking about us, we predict and plan for a better future; Homo sapiens alone can imagine the unobservable; in fact, of everything mentioned so far, this may be the most human quality of all: our ability to daydream, to ponder the mysteries of love and death and the universe around us; we alone can question why flowers smell so pretty and why pooh is so gross and yet sometimes very funny.

So what? Who gives a left breast? Time to cut the cake again: what makes these qualities (and "us") useful?

A quick note, because context is important

here: on planet Earth, extinction is the norm, not the exception; over 99 percent of species that ever roamed the earth are gone, kaput, extinct (yes, you read that correctly, OVER 99 percent, more than, greater than; not good betting odds); violence, hardship, and entropy are the natural orders of the universe; this statement is perhaps best encapsulated in t-shirt format: "Life's a bitch and then you die." Tru dat, shirt.

Fortunately, human beings (and only human beings) possess the qualities necessary to end violence, to overcome adversity, and to create and improve our surroundings. We alone have the potential to foster a moral society, to ensure the greatest happiness for the greatest number of living beings (according to range of conscious experience, of course). We alone can override instinct, imagine a better tomorrow, and do nothing less than change the freaking world.

And so, to answer your question, Mr. Khaki Pants and Golf Shirts, Mr. Drives a $50,000 Car (yes, I saw you; you nearly ran me over that first day), Mr. Wears Too Much Crappy Cologne, Mr. Who Are We to Question What's Right and Wrong, Mr. Always Forgets to Shut Off His Cell Phone Ringer, Mr. the Bible Says an Eye for an Eye, here is my response to your question:

We would measure one another according to the very qualities that make us unique and useful. The proposition that all men are created equal is the biggest bag of bullshit that's ever been served to the general populace (#2 is "innocent until proven guilty," but that is a subject for another time). People have different strengths and different weaknesses; it's time we started calling them like we see them, instead of pussyfooting around.

In a better world, or on a better planet, everyone would be born with the same base value, a number which is infinitely high (based on pure potential); children have the greatest potential and therefore the greatest value; as a person ages, and displays a greater degree of those rare and utilitarian qualities, then he/she would be esteemed or valued more than another person; conversely, as a person ages, and displays traits that go against or detract from these qualities, they would then become less valuable in society's eyes; how much is for the court system to decide (difficult, yes, but not impossible); the court already puts a dollar-value on the loss of human life (let's say due to negligence), and even the loss of limbs, fingers, and toes. These are the scales of human justice, and they demand our most critical thinkers, not a roomful of twelve rejects gathered from the DMV. (No offense, my friends, I included myself in this generalization.)

Would this system be perfect? No. Would it open doors to discrimination? Yes. But at least we could discriminate against the stupid and the violent, as opposed to our current targets: fat, non-white, and gay. But perhaps the greatest improvement we can foresee would be an agreement that a better world (greater happiness and less suffering) is our shared value, responsibility, and motivation--no matter the culture, religion, or politics. Every discussion could begin with that simple acknowledgment.

At this point, I realize that no argument is bulletproof, that I am probably forgetting lots of things, the library is closing and the librarian is yelling at me; I also realize that ultimately people will still believe what they want to believe and hear only what they want to hear, for such is another quirk of human nature; the tenacity with which we hold onto our beliefs is ultimately one of the most curious faults of our design; we are deeply afraid to be wrong and highly reluctant to alter the beliefs we have spent a lifetime acquiring and shaping; we would rather delude ourselves than accept change (This too requires another essay. So many goddamn essays, so little time).

In closing, I feel like I have done my best to answer your question, "How could some people possibly be worth more than others?" I look forward to hearing your response to my response. I'm sure it will be at least as intelligent and eloquent as your parting comment to me, "Opinions are like assholes. Everyone has them, and they all stink."

P.S. After considerable thought, I take back what I said about paying for your dry cleaning bill. If you hadn't stressed me out, I wouldn't have sneezed so vehemently. Lesson learned for you.

A NEW BEGINNING

"What do you mean, it broke?"

"I mean it broke. Busted, somehow."

His words were breathy, forced. Julie was still laying on her stomach atop the dorm-room bed, flattened like a frog; the skin on her back tingled from heat and dampness, Josh's sweat.

"How could it break?"

"I don't know!" then, "Maybe... because I'm so huge."

"Yeah, maybe. Josh this isn't funny. How could this happen?"

"Dude, I have no idea. What? Don't look at me like that."

Julie sat up, swung her legs over the side of the bed; the smell of their sex, usually primal and intoxicating, was instead nauseating, like mushrooms or fungus.

"Ugh! I can't believe this. This is so bad."

"Jules... chillax. It'll be okay."

"Don't use that word. You sound moronic."

"Whatever, just don't freak out. This probably happens all the time."

"No Josh, it doesn't happen all the time.

That's why people use condoms. Because they're supposed to work, like, 99 percent of the time or something."

Julie reached for her cell phone: 12:43 a.m. Saturday, October 21st.

"No birth control is perfect," said Josh.

"Gee thanks," she snapped. "That's helpful."

The world was coming back to her now, her senses returning from vacation, like doors and windows opening, one at a time.

From next door music was blaring, thumping; the music was so loud, why hadn't Julie noticed it earlier? Some cheesy electro-dirty pop, spiked with the distinct laughter of drunk girls.

"Why is that so loud?"

The three candles she'd lit earlier had dwindled to pea-sized balls of light; still, they cast exaggerated, fuzzy shadows on the cinderblock walls; the shadow of her arm could easily reach across the room to the bulletin board above her desk; so Julie pretended to pluck the items hanging there, toss them into the trash.

First went her latest report card (four As, one B, stupid calculus!), followed by the picture of her parents (dad's eyes closed), then a note from Josh "Love you more than cheeseburgers," a list of grad schools with psych programs, then finally the news clippings and blogs from the shooting, the incident which had come to define her, more than anything in her life. Julie was a survivor; or at least, that is what everyone kept telling her.

Josh sat up on the bed. "Maybe we should start, like, using lube or something."

"Yeah, maybe. Good thinking, Josh."

"What? It's got spermicide."

Julie reached for the condom's torn package, studied it. "Josh, these expired last year!"

He leaned in closer, investigating. "They did?

I didn't know! How was I supposed to know?"

"They're your condoms, dummy! Didn't you read the package?"

"Don't call me that. I'm not stupid," then, "Besides if you didn't make me wait so long to have sex, maybe they wouldn't have expired!"

"Ugh! Oh God. You didn't just say that. You really didn't."

"What? What did I say? Julie?"

"Nevermind. I'm going to the bathroom, to see if I can wash this out."

"Sorry! I don't read things. You know that by now."

"Just stop talking please. You're making this so much worse."

Julie marched into the bathroom, closed the door; wet towels hung from the shower rod, the sink, the doorknob; earlier she had asked Josh to freshen up, he still smelled from kickboxing; she leaned into the nearest towel and inhaled; sweat, boy, Josh; why did she love him so much? Does anyone ever get a decent answer to that question? She sighed and turned on the hot water full blast; from next door, the music seemed to pause for a moment, then launch again with renewed fury: techno-beats, DJ/house music; faintly, Julie heard somebody shriek, "Let's dance!" followed by a soft thud and crash.

* * * * *

"Quiz me."

"No."

"Come on. Quiz me."

"No, Josh. Not now. I'm trying to drive."

"Just keep going straight. We're almost there. Quiz me."

She looked at him, found him beautiful again,

as always; maybe it was the smile he kept hidden
behind those gray eyes, poised, ready to please;
or maybe it was his lanky frame, the way his long
arms and legs moved, so fluid and confident.

"Okay, fine. What's combination five?"

"No. No. Start at the beginning."

"What?"

"Start at the beginning. Combo one."

"Josh, are you serious about this?"

"About what?"

"Becoming a cage fighter?"

"Mixed martial artist."

"Oh God, you are serious."

"Jules, I totally knocked out my kickboxing
coach. Left kick to the head. Pow!"

"So you've told me. A dozen times. I just need
to know if this is your plan."

"What do you mean?"

"Is this your plan? Is this our future, Josh?"

"Come on, Jules. Start at the beginning. What's
combination one?"

She drove in silence, searching for the
address. Dead leaves scraped the sidewalk and
collided with vacant storefronts; from the looks
of things, they were in the hood; random dogs
roamed the streets and sidewalks, sniffing for
trash, scraps of food; for the second or third
time, she noticed a pair of shoes or boots,
dangling from the telephone wires above the
street.

"Help me look," she said.

"It's probably right up there, where all those
people are."

Julie saw them too. Up ahead on the right, a
group of ten or twelve adults, brandishing protest
signs; some were sitting, some paced back and
forth. Whenever a car passed by, they shouted
something and waved their signs like pennants.

"Josh," Julie said. "I think that's it."

"What?"

"Planned Parenthood."

As they approached the driveway, Julie slowed the car. The protestors swarmed in, shoving signs in front of the windshield, blocking her view. Aborted fetuses. Tiny arms and legs. Blood. Julie closed her eyes and braked.

"Don't stop," said Josh. "Keep going."

"They're blocking us."

"They'll move, just go."

A knock on the driver's side window, and Julie opened her eyes. A man who looked like Santa Claus peered inside at them, then yelled.

"Abortion is murder!"

"Fuck you!" Josh said. "I'll kick your ass!"

"We're not having an abortion," Julie said, shouting against the glass. "We're just here to get birth control!"

The man backed away from the car, and Julie took advantage to hit the accelerator. The shouting continued as they sped toward the building.

"Murderers!"

"What the fuck?" Josh said. "I mean, seriously?"

Julie didn't respond. Instead she focused on the signs for visitor parking, found an empty spot, and parked. It wasn't until she reached for the door handle that she noticed the spittle on the outside of her window, from the man shouting at them, the angry Santa Claus, so forceful were his words.

*   *   *   *   *

"The sperm inside you are dying right now," the woman said. "By the millions."

Julie nodded, shifted in her chair. "But I read online they can live inside the body for up to five days."

"That's true. But only if they reach the Fallopian tubes. Quite a journey for most sperm."

The nurse gestured to a medical illustration on the wall behind her; a woman's reproductive system, writ en large in pink, yellow, and blue.

"My boys can totally swim," Josh said. "That journey is nothing for them." He snapped his fingers for effect.

"Josh," Julie said, but the nurse continued, unfazed.

"Here's how I usually explain it to people. Each healthy ejaculation contains about 300 million sperm, or about the same number of people living in the United States. Within a few hours, nearly all of them are dead. Only the population of California survives. If you're ovulating, and the entrance to the cervix is open, a number about equal to the residents of Los Angeles will try to swim through there, navigating by heat and chemical signals from the egg. All but a handful will perish in the cervix, attacked by white blood cells or overwhelmed by the journey. On a good day, no, a great day, only about a dozen sperm will make it to Hollywood, the Fallopian tubes."

"Wow," Julie said. "That's, just, hmmm."

"Like I said, if you're ovulating, and there's an egg in the Fallopian tubes, those few remaining sperm will race to fertilize it. If not, they'll rest and wait it out for as long as they can."

"What are the chances," Julie asked, "that an egg is actually there?"

"Statistically, between 1.6 and 3.2 percent. But really, it more depends on when you last had a period, which you said was..."

"About two weeks ago."

"Okay, you're right on the border then."

"Yup," Julie repeated. "Right on the border." The image of the U.S. map stayed in her mind; she wondered which border she was on; all around her, people were dying. By the millions.

"Keep in mind, Julie, even if your timing was perfect, and you've ovulated, and Josh's sperm penetrated the egg, you still might not be pregnant. The fertilized egg still has to travel to the uterus and successfully implant there. Only one out of three fertilized eggs actually do this. And out of those that do implant, another one-third are miscarried."

"Jeez, it's a wonder anyone ever gets pregnant."

"That's why they call it a miracle, I suppose," she paused. "But people get pregnant because people keep trying."

She placed a small box on the table, along with a folder of information titled "Plan B."

"You don't have to take the pill right now. Or even today. But for effectiveness, we do recommend you take it within five days of intercourse."

"Okay," Julie said.

"Nausea is the most common side effect. And headaches. You can read all about it in the packet. And don't be afraid to call us, day or night."

"Okay."

"Any more questions?"

"I don't think so." Julie looked at Josh; the smile was gone from his eyes. He was slumped in his chair, ankles crossed, arms folded. "Josh?"

"What?"

"You ready to go?"

*   *   *   *   *

Her room was clean now; her room was organized! The sheets were washed, the floor swept, the clothes folded and hung, the desk cleared, dusted; and yet still Julie felt the urge to do more; the room would never be clean enough; there was always more to organize; her folders, her closet, drawers, jewelry, makeup.

It reminded her of something the therapist had said, years ago: "The need to organize is almost always related to a feeling of lost control."

In the quad outside her window, Julie could see her corridor-mates playing flip-cup with a group of guys; they were all dressed in long pants, sweatshirts, socks and sandals, trying to savor the last stretch of fall before winter arrived; everybody looked so young to her; they were all just kids.

She lifted the bulletin board from its clips on the wall, decided to refresh it, put up some new pictures. First she un-tacked the sorority photo; why had she even joined?; so stupid; she kept the picture of Josh after his first fight, but moved it to the bottom corner; she imagined him in five years, as a professional kickboxer; his long thin frame would suit him well; he was gorgeous when he moved, so smooth, so patient, and fast; next she un-tacked the photo of her parents, for once grateful that her dad's eyes were closed; she put that picture inside a textbook as a page marker; and then finally, she removed the newspaper clippings: "Man Gunned Down at Local Starbucks," "Shooter Turns Self In," and "Hung Jury Outrages Community."

That which had consumed the past three years of her life; the police statements; interviews with detectives; trial subpoenas; courtroom testimony; the nightmares; the therapy; and always the pity. Everyone pitied Julie; she came to expect that stupid look, heads tilted to one side or another, bottom lip curled down.

No more.

She dug out the candle lighter from a mess of pens and highlighters in the junk drawer and pressed the trigger, testing it; an orange flame erupted at the tip; next she held the newspaper clips over the room's metal trash can and ignited them; black smoke curled from her fingers and she dropped the burning paper into the gray can.

Time for a new beginning; time to make a decision.

The pill itself was surprisingly small, considering its power; she placed the capsule on the dresser and opened a bottle of water.

"Millions of sperm are dying inside you."

She thought of the man outside Planned Parenthood, the one who yelled at her; the one who up until the very last hateful moment, had resembled Santa Claus. She thought of Josh, and how amazing their child would be.

We are the decisions we make.

Julie picked up the pill, took a sip of water. Who was this girl in the mirror?

She touched the glass with her index finger; the reflection reached back toward her, but their fingers did not touch, not exactly; Julie noted a tiny gap between them, the width of the glass itself, a boundary through which neither could pass; "You're right on the border;" how right that woman had been; the two futures of Julie were co-existing at once, based on a chance connection between two microscopic cells; so thin and brief is the window of our possibility.

Julie turned her back on the mirror; there was much to do yet; she would have to re-hang the bulletin board; and start studying for the psych mid-term; then later she will hit the treadmill

and head uptown for some food; before falling
asleep, she'll light some candles and send a
message to Josh, asking him about combination one;
she'll ask him about their future too; and she'll
save the text thread; she'll save everything she
can: words, pictures, memories, every proof of her
existence; she'll savor every moment in this life
she gets, worshipping time itself, like a goddess,
like a lover.

EPILOGUE

MURPHY THE FIRST

Of all the Cerulean myths and legends, none is more celebrated than that of the Council Elder Murphy the First, or Murphy01, as he came to be known.

In the early days of our planet, as with any primitive society, there was much unrest; civil wars were rampant; nations divided amongst nations; brothers fought against brothers; after thousands of years, at long last there came to be two main factions, the Ceruleans and the Krokolvs.

Physically, the Krokolvs were larger and more powerful; the Ceruleans relied on strategy and cunning. Both were strongly devoted to promoting and preserving the highest ideals of their culture; for the Krokolvs, that meant faith; for the Ceruleans, the highest ideal was truth.

Unfortunately, the Ceruleans were greatly outnumbered in those days; though they fought bravely, gradually they found their nation surrounded. And then one night, the Krokolvs used their superior size and sinew to break into the Elders Council building and kidnap the esteemed Cerulean leader, Murphy01.

The king of the Krokolvs predicted (and correctly so) that killing Murphy01 would generate even more sympathy for the Ceruleans; what's more, he realized that Murphy01 was a powerful speaker and certainly the most influential Cerulean of their time; so the king devised a plan to convert Murphy01 to their cause; once the Ceruleans heard their famous leader sing the praises of Krokolvia, the Ceruleans would certainly surrender, and the planet would become theirs.

So the king set about trying to convert Murphy01; as you might expect, this was not an easy task. Time after time, the king failed to do so; Murphy01 was staunch in his conviction that as long as faith was personal in nature, there could be no common ground for a moral code. And so, as the years passed, the king's methods became more and more drastic; when simply starving the Cerulean Elder produced no results, the king had him thrown into a pit of filth and disease. And when that too failed, the king resorted to crude, even barbaric methods of persuasion. What Murphy01 endured at the hands of the Krokolvian king, we may never fully know or understand.

What we do know, is that Murphy01 grew weaker and weaker; his wounds became infected; his body shriveled with malnutrition. Without proper care, the Cerulean would soon die. And so one day Murphy01 summoned the mighty king, promising to recant his views to the entire planet; Murphy01 agreed to say whatever the king wanted him to say; in return, he only asked to spend his remaining, dying days in the Cerulean homeland.

The king, sensing a trick or a ruse on Murphy01's part, agreed to the offer; he even arranged for a ceremony atop the highest mountain on the planet; but for added insurance, the king also devised a foolproof plan to make sure everything went as anticipated.

Soon the day came; all of Krokolvia gathered at the base of the mountain to watch the great Murphy01 renounce his views and bow to their king. The entire world waited, for the fate of the planet was at hand.

First, the guards dragged out Murphy01, emaciated and disfigured; the king wrapped a hibernation blanket around the Elder's shoulders, and raised a claw, silencing the crowd; he then whispered something to Murphy01, causing the Elder to turn and look askance; on the platform nearby stood Murphy01's wife and children, held at knife-point by the guards.

"Choose your words carefully, Murphy the Elder. For I assure you, we will cut their throats right before your eyes. Starting with the youngest."

Murphy01 nodded, solemnly.

"Your audience awaits," said the king. This would be his proudest moment.

Murphy01 stood before them on the platform of the highest mountain; he could feel the strength leaving his body; he focused on this final speech. As the crowd waited, there was silence across the land; you could've heard a slajak drop.

Finally, Murphy01 uttered these infamous words: "Truth, like a child, unites. Faith, like a knife, divides."

And with that, Murphy01 leapt forward, tumbling down the mountainside; his weakened, mangled body arrived at the feet of the madding crowd.

At this point (as with all Cerulean stories) the teller is free to choose his/her/its own ending (you certainly know the end result); but out of the hundreds of endings I've heard, here is the one I like best:

The crowd was incensed; they demanded payback for this trick played upon them, this insult to their faith; so they began chanting, demanding the deaths of Murphy01's family too; some of the Krokolvs even began devouring the Elder's corpse (for such was their custom).

But up on the platform, Murphy01's family began to grieve openly; it gave the king pause; he thought about his own wives and offspring; would they too watch their father die at the hands of the enemy? The thought shook him to his core.

The king bowed down before the Cerulean family. "My guards will escort you home. One day you may return, seeking vengeance. I only ask that you remember this small gesture and have mercy on this old king's soul."

The Krokolv leader then placed his battle sword on the ground at the pincers of the oldest family member; in his distraught state, the youth picked up the sword and raised it high, as if to strike the king.

"No, my son," the mother said, "We are Ceruleans."

It was all she needed to say.

The rueful king lived many years after that, long enough to witness the collapse of his empire. Murphy01's family lived on as well; his sons became esteemed members of the Elders Council; under their guidance, the Ceruleans captured the enemy's capital city without shedding a single drop of Krokolv blood.

As for Murphy01 himself, well, you know what became of him. He is the subject of legends--an eternal symbol of a planet's fierce and blazing hope.

ABOUT THE AUTHOR

Nominated for a XXXVI Pushcart Prize, as well as two "Best of the Net" collections, Pat Pujolas has been featured in *Outsider Writers*, *Connotation Press*, *Heartlands Today*, and *Writer's Digest* (as a winner of the 1994 Short Story Competition). He's also credited with two episodes of MTV's animated series "3-South." This is his first work of published fiction. Originally from Cleveland, Pujolas has also lived in San Francisco, Seattle, Hood River, Los Angeles, and coastal Maine; currently he resides in Akron, Ohio, with his wife and kids. To contact him: pat.pujolas@gmail.com

INTERVIEW WITH THE AUTHOR

[*Connotation Press* Fiction Editor Meg Tuite
talks to Pat Pujolas about the short story
"Jimmy Lagowski Saves the World"]

*Q: This story is heart-wrenching and masterfully
written. You've chosen to move from present to
flashbacks, which seems to me the perfect form for
this story and told so directly and with so little
emotion that it blasts out of the reader instead!
Did you have a plan while you wrote this story?*

A: Yes, I definitely had a plan, which like all my
plans, failed miserably. But it's important to
adjust your initial plans as obstacles come up,
and more importantly, as better plans suggest
themselves. This is how writing has always worked
for me; at the onset I think I know the story I am
telling, until the characters themselves begin
taking over, choosing their own courses of action,
and dictating their own fates; by the time I'm
finished writing, the story is quite different
from the original intent (and almost always
better). For example, the original first line of

this story was "They called each other douchebag..." and the story took place entirely in the past, ending with the tragic fire. But as the narrative unfolded, I realized Dagmar was giving Jimmy the advice that would one day save his life. So I kept writing.

Q: There is this deep, yet unspoken relationship between the narrator, Jimmy, and his childhood friend, Dagmar. They share this alternate world that the narrator has created to help survive the pain of finding themselves somewhat helpless in an "adult" world. What was your inspiration for "The Ceruleans?"

A: Essentially this is a story about escape; in the past, Dagmar is seeking to escape an abusive relationship with her stepfather; in the present Jimmy quite literally wants to shed his own skin, to escape the prison of his deformed appearance; both situations invoke feelings of helplessness, and the Ceruleans provide the means to escape, temporarily at first (spoken word), then permanently (written word).

The inspiration for this entire story, along with the Ceruleans, began several years ago in conversations I had with a close family member, who is now deceased. Like Jimmy, this person was injured in a fire, which led to multiple health problems. And like Jimmy, this young man was extraordinarily creative. Every holiday or family get-together, he would tell me stories about a planet he imagined that was ruled by mutant insects (Prez Mantis, Major Roach, and Sergeant Ant). So, I guess in real life, I am Dagmar, encouraging him to write those stories down; of course, in real life things don't always turn out the way you'd hoped; that is instead the role of fiction.

As an aside, I really do like the word "cerulean." There is a music to it, I think, those four syllables strung together in succession (sah-ROOL-ee-an). It makes me feel calm.

Q: And I love the starfish motif that comes back again and again! It's very much a symbol to me as a reader. Outstanding! Do you have a writing schedule and if so, any tricks that seem to work for you best?

A: No, and no. I'm definitely not an example for young writers to follow (or any writers for that matter). In the past I've tried writing 1,000 words per day (or more); I've tried writing at the same times every day (mostly mornings); but now, having an additional full-time job and three children, I am schedule-challenged and trick-free. So when I do make time to write (whether it's ten minutes or several hours), I write passionately, furiously. The only rule I consistently follow: write each piece as if it's the last thing you'll ever write. Somehow that works for me and my lack of process/routine.

Q: Do you write short stories exclusively or have you attempted writing a novel and/or poetry?

A: I've written one novel, two screenplays, a memoir (based on three cross-country journeys), two television scripts, one collection of short stories, and numerous other short pieces. So far, only a few of these things have made it to publication or production; and trust me, that's a good thing! Every time I write a new piece, I learn something; and so when I look back on prior works, I see their enormous, gaping flaws.

Q: Wow, okay, you just blew me away on that answer! You're a multi-media Cerulean! Who would you say are the biggest influences on your writing career?

A: Mostly other authors, whose work spoke to me at a particular time of my life. Currently, it's Haruki Murakami (specifically "The Wind-Up Bird Chronicles"); in the past it's been John Updike, Kurt Vonnegut, Timothy O'Brien, Joyce Carol Oates, Annie Proulx, David Foster Wallace, Denis Johnson, and others I'm forgetting right now. They influenced me to become a writer, by enriching my experience as a human being, and by setting the quality bar high enough to encourage relentless improvement.

Q: What are you reading at this time?

A: "Memory Wall" by Anthony Doerr (of course!). I just finished this year's Pen/O.Henry collection, as well as a book on perceptual errors by Jim Hallinan. I read a lot of literary fiction (recent faves: "Super Sad True Love Story" by Gary Shteyngart, "Await Your Reply" by Dan Chaon, and "The Illumination" by Kevin Brockmeier) as well as scientific non-fiction (in particular, I love reading about the human brain, its functions and malfunctions, injuries and disorders, anomalies, etc). Last, I enjoy surfing fiction sites like *Connotation Press* (nobody paid me to write this!) to discover raw talent and fresh, original voices.

A CAUSE-FRIENDLY BOOK

Just when you thought this book couldn't get any more awesome... Kapow! It does. The author is donating 10 percent of all royalties (after the printer, publisher, and Amazon take their cuts) to the burn center of a leading children's hospital. Their legal department prohibits me from mentioning the name (lest I profit off their reputation), but let's just say it rhymes with "miners" and may or may not have a facility in Cincinnati, Ohio. So there you have it. In summary: buy more books, help more kids. Peace, my friends.

Made in the USA
Lexington, KY
20 March 2012